MY DEAREST
Mackenzie

MY DEAREST
Mackenzie

rachel blaufeld

Books by
rachel blaufeld

Romance that will break your heart and mend it with the promise of everlasting love.

Second Chance at Love Series
The Back Nine
The Second Half

Grand Love Series
Grand Escape
Love is Grand

World of True North Series
Friendzoned

Stand Alone Titles
Break Point
To See You
Heart Stronger
Hot for His Girl
Wanderlove
Love Disregarded

Love at Center Court Series
Vérité
Dolce

CHAPTER One

MACK

My Dearest Mackenzie—

*If you're reading this...**well then, you know.** I've gone and crossed over to the dark side.*

I always was a fan of those movies...remember when you were younger, and we went to see them in the theaters? Of course you do!

I know you're probably upset with me, and I'm sorry I didn't tell you about the melanoma. Truly.

One day I was fine, and the next, I was dying. Honestly, I didn't believe Dr. Hall at first. And then I didn't want to bother anyone. I've always felt life is for the living, and there was no reason to interrupt everyone's regularly scheduled programming with sadness and worry.

There's nothing more to say now (because I'm gone).

My one hope is that you won't forget me. Please. I'm rambling, but one thing is for certain: I never imagined leaving you this soon. When your grandpa had a heart attack when you were ten, I figured I'd be a widow for a long time, watching you grow older, fall in love, and maybe bring a little one into the world yourself. I always believed I'd live to be a great-grandmother!

Now that I'm gone, I want you to think about how I made you soup when you were sick or homemade fried chicken fingers when you were sad. It was a labor of love, and I hope you bring the same sort of compassion to your own life and those who you hold close.

Remember going to an R-rated movie when your dad wouldn't let you see one? That was exhilarating and the type of excitement you should assign to everyday doldrums.

Bend the rules, my dearest. Don't let anyone tell you that you can't do something.

As I write this, I don't know what it's like up in the sky, but if it's possible to miss something or someone, you can be sure I miss you the most.

You, my dear grandson, were the bright spot in many of life's bleary moments. Being your grandmother was my greatest treasure. Sure, I love your cousins, but you were my golden angel. My chance to do it all better, correct the mistakes I made with your dad. We all know Susie wasn't meant to be molded, and I did the best I could with her, but your dad got caught up in something he shouldn't have. I don't mean your mom; I mean my baggage and me. It was me who haunted him. You won't ever understand, but I promise you—it was me.

As for Samantha, I wish your mom well, but her missing out on life with you was a deficit she could never make up for in my mind. I wasn't a substitute, but I'm sure glad I was there for you. These are the experiences, moments, and snippets I never would give up.

The past few years, I know you've been building your career and learning to be out on your own, and I only wish you could have spent more time at home, so I could watch. Although spreading your wings, launching new products, expanding the company, it's all important, and I know you're exceeding all expectations. Like when you surprised yourself as the kicker on your football team. Those guys were your brothers and extended family, and you did not disappoint them. It's time to create a new family...

I made myself a big pot of mishy-mashy soup today, and I couldn't help but think of you and wanted to remind you of a few things before I left this world.

1. *Find love and hold on to it. Not like your dad, who drowned in it. That was my fault...there were a lot of reasons why I didn't give him what he needed, and he sought it elsewhere and from the wrong person. It wasn't until too late that he realized he was caught in an undertow. Except we got you out of the bad deal, and when you find love, don't scrounge it like so many others. Nurture it like a man who values what he's discovered.*

2. *Love has a mind of its own, so remember, nine times out of ten, the woman (or man, whoever floats your boat, grandson) is right. The universe speaks, and you need to listen.*

3. *Stop trying to make peace with your mom. She is happy doing whatever she's doing, and you are a wonderful young man despite her. Her loss.*

4. *Flush the toilet. Always. The saying if "it's yellow, let it mellow" from your football days is simply wrong.*

5. *Health starts in the kitchen. Takeout or delivery junk, or whatever you kiddos eat today is the road to making unhealthy choices. Limit your booze too.*

6. *Do NOT ever visit me in the cemetery. What a waste of time. Live your life to the fullest.*

Aren't you glad I made you learn to read and write in cursive?

I love you.

Grammy Milly

I stared at the flowing words on the crinkled piece of paper, knowing every single letter without reading it. The cursive dribble had been living rent-free in my head and at the bottom of my sock drawer—*like my football days*—for the last twenty years. Leave it to Milly to haunt me today; it was just like her to captivate me when I least wanted it.

I'd not done a single thing on her list other than remember her and the moments we shared. About once a month, whether I tried to avoid it or not, I thought about what item she would be most upset about— my seeking out my good-for-nothing mother (repeatedly, until I gave it a permanent rest), or my total lack of caring when it came to finding love. Maybe the way I'd visited her tombstone a million times and carefully placed flowers? Or perhaps my notorious bachelor habits. I rarely flushed when I drained the dragon, and I lived on a rotation of delivery service meals. Sometimes I screwed the chef, but I tried not to. *Why?* Because I didn't do leftovers. Sexy cooks aside, my grandmother meant well in her advice, but she had to know these sorts of things were unattainable for a man like me. None of this meant I was a bad guy or mean person. In fact, if anything, I was protecting my softie heart from a lifetime of disappointment.

At least that's what I told my friend, Teddy, when he called, reminding me of the letter and his similar wishes…

Thankfully, my phone buzzed, and it wasn't my aforementioned friend.

Knocking me out of my reverie, I was grateful for the distraction.

I hit the button and accepted the call, hearing my name ring through the speaker.

"Mack!"

"What's up, Corey?" It came out gruff, but a perpetual frog stuck in my throat left me hoarse throughout the day. My assistant knew this fun fact about me, and I was sure paid it no mind.

Corey also happened to be obsessive and easily excited on his worst day; when he was having a good day, his exuberance was obscene. My mood barely ever registered on him through his own jubilation.

"There is some woman here, Frances is her name. Wait, what? My apologies…"

I imagined him flapping his lips as fast as he could. *Hallelujah*, his work was impeccable.

Corey trailed off in the background, mumbling to the mysterious woman. "I'm here, sorry, Frankie is her name. And she's here to see you, boss."

"Hmmm? Did I miss an appointment?"

"No, no, you didn't miss a thing. She doesn't have one."

Tugging my French cuffs down and inserting the cuff link in the holes while my phone sat on the dresser, I tried to remember if I knew a Frances or a Frankie.

"Do we have business with her?" I was already on my second cuff link, and five steps ahead in my day. We had a ribbon cutting at a new store, and afterward I was meeting with a bergamot supplier in town.

"She won't say. All she said is she needs to see you. 'The Mr. Mackenzie Miller' was how she referred to you."

"Corey, I hope this isn't some dramatic plan of yours to set me up." I growled the last part into the phone. A few times over the last several years, Corey got it in his mind that I needed a happily-ever-after and added me to dating sites. "The last time, I fired you."

"You were kidding. You couldn't live without me. But, yes, yes, I still took you seriously."

I could live without Corey, but it wasn't worth the energy explaining that to my needy assistant.

"No, it's not a fix-up. Frances, I mean Frankie, walked right in here this morning, somehow dusted right past security, sped into the elevators and straight up to the top floor, asking to see you."

I could tell Corey lowered his voice and was attempting to be private, but imagined he wasn't as stealthy as he thought he was.

Snagging my money clip off the top of my dresser, I shoved it in my pocket and walked out of my massive bedroom. The smell of coffee dragged me down the hall toward the kitchen.

"As you're aware, I'm off to Westchester this morning for an opening there. The car is getting me here, and I won't be back until lunchtime. And then I have meetings. So if Miss…what is this woman's last name?"

Stealing a mug from the cabinet and pouring a healthy dose of coffee, I waited while Corey asked.

"Miss Will-Tell-You-When-She-Meets-You. Her words, not mine."

"For fuck's sake, I'm forty-six and graying by the minute. I don't have time for these games. Have her make an appointment. I think I'm booking for October."

I disconnected the call without any further conversation spent on this ridiculous woman and what was more than likely Corey's hijinks.

Double-checking my phone was in silent mode, I made sure it was June and laughed to myself. October was a long way off for Miss Will-Tell-You-When-She-Meets-You to wait.

Oh well.

*A*s I climbed into the black SUV idling outside my building, I remembered the exact moment I'd received the call about my grandmother dying. I'd graduated from a very prominent business school—based on my own merit and not my family's name—almost a year to the day, and I was working myself to the bone, climbing the ranks at a shitty, albeit huge cosmetics company, hoping my dad would let me come on board at the family business soon. At twenty-six, my only goal was proving myself worthy enough for my father, turning out better than my mom ever imagined, and being richer than anyone I knew. To me, money and notoriety and success were the ultimate companions. People became too messy, involving themselves where they were not wanted, and were largely unreliable. Other than one friend in college, who forced me under his wing, I'd had no one to lean on. Ever.

My dad had delivered the news about Milly as if it was the daily sales conference call. Those two always had beef, but my dad couldn't run the business and raise me at the same time, so he leaned on my grandmother, allowing her involvement when it came to me.

Currently seated in the back of my chauffeured SUV, as we hit the highway my mind traveled back to Grammy's funeral. Ironically, today was mostly about her. Tears no longer came when I thought of the feisty old lady who helped raise me. But on the day of her burial, I cried when I slipped into my car. I still drove myself back then—in the car gifted to me by my father.

Later that week, after the funeral, the lawyer who managed Milly's estate handed me the infamous letter and access to a sizable trust. I would never forget my aunt, Susie, eyeing the envelope, and later asking me what it was. I'd replied, "Oh, nothing. Silly nothings," when she'd asked, not admitting I'd welled up again reading it.

That same evening, over a double Lagavulin, I couldn't help but think how Grammy handed out her advice without strings; I wondered why the trust wasn't connected to my doing the tasks in her letter. Probably because she knew I wouldn't ever follow through.

Now, in the present moment, at a godforsaken mall, I did the only thing I knew how to do when it came to my grandmother—honor her name. Here I was, dedicating another store to the woman. Carrying on her legacy was the best I could do. It was more than my aunt or dad ever did, so I considered it a win as I entered the mall with a squadron of magazine and newspaper journalists following me.

After the ribbon cutting and obligatory pictures, I stood in the hallway and admired the storefront.

"Hey, hey, Mr. Mackenzie, hey, Mr. Miller, excuse me." A shorter blond with all the right curves and an even more fabulous smile yanked on my arm.

I wasn't immune to advances, but this didn't feel much like a come-on. More like a summons to stand in front of a jury. "I'm sorry, but a little space, please." I spoke softly. Of course, this tiny female wasn't an imminent risk to me, but I never wanted to be viewed as one to her. Closeness sometimes equaled threat, my Southern gentleman of a coach told us in college, and I'd taken it to heart. Somewhere deep in my dark soul, I was a gentleman.

The petite woman took a step backward, but then firmly planted herself and eyed me up and down. Her hair was ironed straight, the smallest curl starting to perk up by her ear, the telltale signs she'd blown out her waves. A small huff of breath released from her mouth before she spoke. "Mr. Miller," she said as if this was a pertinent matter.

"Mack, not Mr. Miller. That was my dad. And honestly, never Mackenzie. Ever," I corrected her, thinking this must be my infamous visitor from the morning. "Frances, I assume." I felt my eyebrow raise.

"Frankie to almost everyone. Frances Burns." She held out her hand.

I slid my hand in hers—the gesture meant to be professional, yet it felt more provocative than an invitation to jump into bed together. Something scintillating wafted between us, and I waved it away with my imagination. I didn't mix business and pleasure.

"What can I do for you, Miss Burns?" I returned my hand to my side.

"Congratulations. I'm sorry to barge in on your party, but your assistant scheduled me for October, and that simply wasn't going to work."

"You seem to be barging into several places today. My office, the mall. Where's next?"

A sliver of a smile crept up her face, and there were a few crinkles on the sides of her eyes. As I watched her chest rise and fall, I tried to calculate how old Frances Burns was. I'd put my money on thirty-eight…maybe -nine.

"Nowhere, thanks. I found what I was looking for…"

"Did you want to try the perfumery? I know they're booked for a few weeks, but judging by your stalking tendencies, I could arrange for you to go. You know, so you don't harass the manager."

Milly's Perfume Lounge was fully my concept, and if I was truly honest, my baby. I'd turned my family's skin care line into the top of the luxury cosmetics totem pole, and then started adding beauty outposts in high-end malls and shopping areas. First was Silky Skin, and now Milly's, whose fifth store was opening today in Westchester. My dad never believed in the idea all the way to his deathbed, but I wasn't up for thinking about him today.

"No. I mean, it looks lovely, but that's not what I came for. It seems you and I have mutual history, and—"

"Have we met?" I was starting to become equal parts intrigued and annoyed. I needed to get back to the city, but this woman had me mesmerized for no reason whatsoever.

"We haven't met," she said while scrunching her brow. "My grandpa recently died, and he left the world carrying a torch for your grandmother."

Now I was beginning to think this woman was taking me for a fool, which I certainly was anything but.

"You mean, my grandmother, who this store behind me is named for?" I half turned, catching a glimpse of the Tiffany blue speckled exterior, the store name written in cursive across the top. It was meant to look whimsical and classy at the same time.

"Your grandma, Rose Miller, who, I know from Google, your family called Milly. But my grandfather referred to her as 'my Rosie.'"

"Listen, Frances—Frankie—it's been nice of you to find me, but I can promise you I never once heard anyone call my grandmother Rosie. In fact, she would've probably punched them in the jaw, let alone someone who added *my* before Rosie."

I took a closer look at the woman in front of me, wearing a pencil skirt and coral-colored blouse. Her green eyes were carefully made up and lips a shade lighter than the silk in her top—hey, I worked in makeup. "Maybe on another day, a different time or place, we would have hit it off, but using my grandmother as bait is a firm no from me." I turned to walk away, and I'll give it to the peanut, she grabbed the fabric of my suit.

"Can't you at least listen to me? I've been trying to get in touch with you for weeks."

I stared at where her manicured hand clasped onto my arm, a million retorts running through my head, including something about the cost of the suit. Then, a look in her eyes, something far-off or nostalgic, caught me and I sucked back any agitation.

"Why don't we go to my car? And you can meet with me there and tell me about your grandfather and this Rosie theory. My driver, Alex, will be with us, so it's safe."

A visible sigh of relief flowed out of her chest, and I watched her fingers slide away from me. "I'm not worried about you. I do kickboxing."

That was her response. Seriously, she did kickboxing.

All I could manage was a nod, and I started moving toward the exit.

Outside the mall, Alex had the SUV idling, and before he had a chance to get out I opened the door and slipped in to the far seat. "So you don't have to slide," I explained to my guest.

Frankie hoisted her tiny frame into the mammoth vehicle and sat in the seat next to me.

"Alex, this is Miss Burns. She has some information for me. Feel free to stay or go get a coffee. Frankie does kickboxing, so we are safe and sound."

"Are we done with that joke?" Frankie asked me while half turning in her seat so she could meet my gaze. "I know you're mocking me and I don't appreciate it, soccer boy."

"Football," I corrected her.

"Only because you were the kicker thanks to your soccer skills, tough guy."

She had me there. For the second time, all I could manage was a nod.

"The internet, sorry. I've been trying to find a connection to link me to you for a while." She gave a halfhearted explanation for her information gathering.

"I'm thinking you couldn't find one, so you went with harassment instead?"

I'd give it to the pint-sized blond. She didn't back down, only shined a slow smile on me, and said, "It was necessary."

A quiet beat passed between us, neither of us winning the showdown.

Alex took advantage of the peaceful moment and slipped out of the SUV.

"Look, I'm sorry about your grandfather. I don't recognize the last name Burns. I'm sure he meant a lot to you. Nonetheless, I just don't see how this connects us." I decided to get this whole discussion over with, so onward it was. I ran a hand through my hair, noting it needed to be trimmed. I'd call my stylist to come over to the office this week.

"Thank you. He was a very kind man," my new friend acknowledged. "His name was James Burns. Jimmy to all his friends, and Paps to family. My dad is James Jr., and I was supposed to be…wait for it…James the

Third. Surprise…I was a girl! I was named Frances for my maternal grandmother, and called Frankie by my dad and Paps because I was the tomboy they always wanted."

Despite being focused on her story and family history, I did take pause when she mentioned tomboy; she certainly didn't look like any buddy of mine.

"Are you listening?" She was intuitive, I'd give her that.

"Yes. While I'm glad you felt the need to share, I'm not sure what your family tree has to do with me. I have my own. Do you want to know?" I was being snarky, but this all seemed a bit superfluous. "I'll fill you in. My grandmother and grandfather, Rose and Harold Miller, gave birth to my dad, Jake Miller, and his sister, Susie. Jake married Samantha for a quick cup of coffee and had me. Samantha appropriately named me after her favorite soap opera star because that's what women who don't really have any emotional ties to their child do. She didn't wait long to split. Most of that you can read on the internet, except for the splitting and soap opera bit. Those facts have mostly been scrubbed from my history. I'd appreciate you not sharing that little fact."

She nodded, casting her gaze to the floorboard, her long eyelashes accentuated by a coat of mascara. The strange but fascinating woman appeared deep in thought, giving me pause. Not sure why I'd dumped all that information on her; sharing the history of my name was deeper than I went with anyone since Teddy, and he and I were teammates. It wasn't the type of information I spread around freely, let alone with strangers.

Ha, Teddy…no one busted my balls like him. I hadn't thought about the guy in a while. I made a mental note to reach out to him.

"Look," Frances spoke, bringing her gaze to meet mine, "are you listening?"

"To your personal mission to resurrect your grandfather's love affair? Only half—"

"None of this is easy for me to say. It's clear your grandmother never mentioned my Paps, and that stings. Fact is, he spoke about her a lot. 'Rosie, the one who got away…'"

Clearing my throat, I stopped her from going on. "This is nonsense. Did you hear me say my mother didn't raise me? S.P.L.I.T. My grandmother stepped in, and she never once mentioned your Paps, as you call him. She was married to my grandfather and died never loving anyone else. If you want money or a payout, or I don't know what, this isn't the place to get it."

"But—"

"I'm going to have to ask you to step out of the vehicle now."

I felt a twinge in the back of my neck. It was the spot where stress always hit me, and I didn't need this shit today. What I needed was a new bergamot supplier and a stiff cocktail, and now, a massage.

"It was nice meeting you, Ms. Burns, but our time is up. Again, I'm sorry about your grandfather."

Her smile now a full-on frown, she opened the door and set one foot outside. "I have a few things I could show you."

She half turned to look at me with her doe eyes, and I almost acquiesced, but I didn't need any more deadbeats coming out of my past. I'd stuffed my mom firmly in the back of my mind, and this James or Jimmy dude wasn't making an appearance in my world. "No thanks. Have a good day."

Frances didn't look back. With her loss of pride rippling off her, she stepped fully out of the SUV and shut the door in my face. There was an idiot born every day, and I wasn't one. No way I was falling for a con.

Thank whoever was up there in the sky, Alex appeared out of thin air and got into the driver's seat. Being the man I'd come to respect, he didn't ask any questions.

On our way back to the city, I made another mental note to discuss boundaries with Corey. No more visitors or setups or pranks or whatever this blasphemy was…

MACK

*L*ater that week, my aunt Susie called. She didn't touch base often, and when she did, it was when she wanted or needed something. It was Friday and I was looking forward to a golf weekend, and I knew it was about to be soured.

"Hi, Mack. How are you?" I heard the traffic honking in the background.

"Fine. What's up, Susie?" I got right to the point. It never seemed like what she really wanted, but Susie had sold her shares in the company to my dad when her husband, Arthur, wanted to invest in real estate. They'd been successful, and I was grateful to not have to work with her or her two brunette, curly-haired, and "freckled from too many vacations in the Caymans" daughters—Sonya and Sylvia. They were both pains in my ass, always wanting something like their mom.

"I wanted to know if you were coming for the Jewish New Year. Did you see my email on it? As I said, Sylvia and Tom have included some friends this year, so you may enjoy meeting a few people your age?"

I'd seen the email, glanced at it and trashed it. It had popped into my inbox after the Frances Shakedown, as I'd come to think of the other day.

To the innocent, Susie's invite might seem innocent and kind, but I knew it had a nefarious bent. "I'm not sure," I told my aunt. "It's three months away, Susie, but I'll probably have a quiet meal at home."

In reality, I'd do what I always did. I'd visit Milly's grave, come home, and watch a livestream service over a bowl of takeout matzo ball soup. It wasn't grand or even close to any tradition, but it was my own annual plan.

"That's a shame. You shouldn't be alone. It's a holiday. Plus, Tom's colleague is looking to launch a product in the skin care world. I thought the two of you could meet. She's also single…and Jewish."

Boom! There it was. My dad's only sister coming in hot with a two-for-one. A potential wife with a long-term interest in my company.

"Tom was thinking of backing Traci. That's her name. Traci Wechsler. Beautiful, strawberry blond hair, thin, went to Cornell. Come to think of it, she goes to the Hamptons on the weekends often. You should come out and meet her."

I felt my head shaking side to side to the nonsense, my brain in overdrive on how to respond. My sort-of venture capitalist cousin-in-law, Tom, had been wanting to sink his teeth into my financially secure business for a while. "That's so nice of you to think of me and the company, but I try not to do business with friends of family. It just feels more like a potential catastrophe than a safe zone. And I'm not dating anyone other than my job at the moment."

"Milly would want you to come. Not just for the holiday but out to the beach house too," Susie screamed over an ambulance whirring by. I imagined her sitting straight as an arrow, in the back of an SUV, privacy screen up, her black hair plastered into a bob, and not even glancing out the window to see what the emergency might be.

I laughed. "Milly wanted me to fall in love with some serendipitous person I met like in a movie, not a financial prospect of Tom's. Thanks for the invite though." I rolled my eyes at the thought of Milly believing the universe would send someone fascinating and worthy my way. I was a lot of things; lucky wasn't one of them.

I disconnected the call and decided to go for a run outside. Best part of building a shower in my office was escaping to the nearby Hudson River Trail for a midday pounding of the pavement. By the time I returned with five miles on my feet and a clearer head, I'd forgotten Susie and Tom's proposition and was ready to face the last few hours of my work week. It wasn't often I took a weekend away from it all, but when I did, I did.

"Mack?" Corey poked his head in my office as I resecured my cuff link.

"You can go. Get out," I instructed him, assuming he wanted to start his free weekend early. I wasn't sure who was more excited about my weekend off, Corey or me.

"No, it's not that." He cleared his throat and stepped into my office slowly.

"What? It's not like you to be bashful. Spit it out," I told my assistant who was staring at me like he'd seen Santa Claus, for real.

"She's here. Again."

"Who is here? Susie? I just spoke with her."

"Not Susie." Corey approached with a caution I rarely saw him exhibit. "I know in the past I've played a few jokes or tried to set you up. But I heard you the other day—no more. I don't even know how she is getting past security—"

"Cookies. Oatmeal chocolate chip, to be specific," rang through my office, the one and only Frances Burns strutting right in as if she belonged.

"Definitely not Susie, although I might prefer her." I turned toward Corey before quickly focusing on our visitor. "Hello, Ms. Burns. I'm not a big oatmeal chocolate chip fan."

"Good thing I didn't save you any."

I couldn't help the small smile spreading across my face. The tiny blond half-pint had nerve, I'd say. "What brings you back to stalk me?"

"Remember, I kickbox," she sassed back.

I felt Corey's head pinging between the two of us. "I certainly do. Now tell me, what can we do for you?"

She stood there perfectly still until I noticed a small twitch in her neck. She seemed to be motioning between Corey and the door.

"Do you want privacy? You have to use your words." She actually glared at me, and my smile grew wider. "Now Frances, do you need to speak with me alone?"

"I do." She jutted her chin out and stood as tall as her frame would allow.

"Corey, I know you would prefer to get out the popcorn and enjoy the show, but I'll be okay. Promise."

Poor Corey tucked tail and headed out, but not before turning and winking at me. If I didn't know better, I'd think he planned this. But after the ass ripping I'd given him on his pranks, there was no way he'd risk it.

As soon as he left, I turned toward my visitor. "Now Frances, I'm heading out for the weekend soon. So what business do we have left to discuss? I thought we were all done." I ran my hand through my hair and noted it was still a bit damp from my shower. My mind screamed to get out of this discussion as fast as possible. On the contrary, my body didn't care how inappropriate it was to imagine Little Miss Kickboxing in the shower with me. Yep, that was where my head went. *The other one.*

"I'm sorry for how the other day went...excuse me, do you hear me?"

I nodded, leaving my shower fantasies where they belonged—not in this room.

"Like I said, I'm sorry, but I need you to understand how important this is to me. My Paps—"

"Frances."

"Frankie, please. The way you say it sounds old. No, no, dirty. I don't know. It's just Frankie to everyone."

She had me at dirty, but I got back on track. "Frankie, listen, I know your Pap must've been special. I get that. My grandmother was a force herself. But he's gone, like my Grammy is, and we can't bring them back. All we can do is think of them, remember the good times with them, and live our lives."

"It's Paps. And there is a connection with us. At least a history we should find out about. He loved her. *His Rosie.*"

"There is no history," I barked back, but my mind swirled with explanations. Milly always talked about true love. Maybe there was a deeper meaning?

Frances, aka Frankie, looked at me dead-on, her eyes blazing into mine—deep green forests beckoning me to hike around and explore, like the mountains of New Hampshire in graduate school.

"It's normal to want some sort of closure when someone dies. It's clear to me that you and your grandfather were extremely close, and he told you whatever he told you for some reason. It's not my place to speculate why, but I do know it wasn't so you would come and try to tangle me up in your emotional mess."

"What if…I don't know…the what-ifs are endless, and I can't let it go."

Clearing the toad in my throat, I swallowed my pride and over four decades of feelings. "I have to let it go. You see, I've spent a lifetime living in what-ifs. What if my dad didn't get tangled up with my shit mom? What if I didn't have Milly? What if I didn't prove myself in my business? I'm not about to open another big can of what-ifs in my life. Period. End of subject."

I said the last part with a hint of anger and a rumble in my chest. Did this deter Frances Burns? No.

She walked steadfastly toward me and, without asking or even questioning if it was all right with her nonverbals, took my hand in hers. This pint of a woman was worse than any reporter; she opened doors that had been bolted shut since the day Milly passed.

"Mackenzie, it's okay to feel with me. That's what I want. I need to explore what happened with my Paps, and I know you're fighting the idea but I sense you want to also."

Her skin was smooth and electric against mine, my head and body in a world war. "No, I don't want to explore anything but my golf weekend, which you are making me late for. So if you'll excuse me, Ms. Burns, I need to go."

"My Paps played golf. Not very well, but he liked the idea of it. A gentleman's sport, he called it."

"Again, very sweet, but I have to go." My mouth was saying one thing, yet my hand was still entwined with Frankie's.

I quickly extracted my fingers, but she rambled on. "That was my Paps. A gentleman. He believed in fairness, shaking hands, and being honest."

Stepping back, I looked down at Frances and raised an eyebrow. "If that's what you call dangling a carrot, making up lies, or oversharing tidbits from the past with your impressionable granddaughter."

She crossed her arms in front of her, forcing me to notice the pink satin camisole she wore under her ivory blazer. It had a small bit of lace trim by the cleavage, and I couldn't help but note she was not lacking in that area…

"Eyes up here, Mr. Miller."

Raising my hands in the air, I admitted my guilt. "Look, I really have to go."

"Will you think about taking a quick peek at what I have? We can meet somewhere neutral. A coffee shop, a bar, or wherever you pick."

It took every muscle in my body to keep from saying, *If you wear that pencil skirt, I'll meet you anywhere…* But that wasn't the man Milly raised me to be.

"I can't. I'm sorry, Frances, but I can't. My dad is gone. My grandmother is gone. Lord knows where my mother is…no sense in lying to you about that since you seem to be a truth serum for me. This company, my family's name, is all I have. I am not about to go trekking on an expedition that would change any of that."

"Here," she said while stomping her foot. "Take this." She shoved a business card at me and spat out, "When you change your mind, call me. I know you will." She spun and walked out faster than I could reply.

"I won't" was what I whispered to her ass as she sashayed out the large mahogany door, paying no mind to me or my misgivings.

Turning the card in my hand, I read her name aloud, as if I didn't know it. *Ms. Frankie Burns*

It listed the store where she worked—one of New York's finest and oldest.

Men's Department

I'd bet she made a killing. Between her deadly looks and smart wit, she was likely to capture the heart of every shopping male in a ten-mile radius.

By Appointment Only

This meant she was pretty damn excellent at her job. And spent all her time around men; she knew how to handle and manipulate the Y chromosome. It figured; she sold suits to overeager men. One glance at her and you would know any man with a taste for women would be a goner. Even when she ran off at the mouth, she was the perfect combination of sexy, sultry, and cute.

"I'm going to head out." Corey poked his head in, jolting me from a fantasy of being fit for a suit by the one and only Frances. It did sound a little dirty coming from me…

"I thought you left."

"And miss the show?" He half smirked, partially smiled at me.

"I'm warning you," I told him to no avail.

"That one packs a punch, and apparently packs a mean cookie. I called down to security and told them not to fall for her baked goods anymore."

"Well, at least you did one right thing today."

"I don't think it's me you have to worry about, boss. Pretty sure the blond-haired pipsqueak who keeps weaseling her way into your life is the one you need to look out for."

For the second time today, someone turned and strode out of my office, not allowing me a chance to reply.

"She is. She is." I spoke to the back of Corey's large frame, hoping he didn't hear me admit the truth.

CHAPTER *Three*

FRANKIE

amn that asshole, I couldn't help myself from thinking. It had been a few days since Mackenzie "call me Mack" Miller had unceremoniously asked me to leave his car. *The nerve!* Our conversation was over, according to him, and I was expected to jet away gracefully.

My thoughts were going wild as I smoothed my hand down the front of my camisole. Staring at myself in the mirror as I got ready for work, my mind wandered to a thousand different places. I took in how my early summer tan contrasted with the pale pink fabric of my suit, while I examined my abdomen. Turning to the side, I breathed out heavy, pushing and puffing my stomach as far as it would go, which wasn't much at all. To most, my obsession probably seemed seated in my work in fashion and style. I knew otherwise.

It had been close to eight years since my life took a screeching turn, yet I still checked for a pooch. My deflated belly only mocked me. If it could speak, it would ask why I keep doing this… Alas, my stomach didn't talk.

And I wasn't a great listener, so case closed.

Snagging my coffee cup from the dresser, I walked into the bathroom and took my last slug before applying Silky's Bar-Bay pink lipstick. Sealing the cap back on the tube, I scolded myself for even buying it, let alone wearing it.

It had been about three weeks since I'd first visited an actual Silky Skin store. Of course, I'd known all about the cosmetics and skin care line, but I wanted to see everything for myself before heading to meet Mackenzie Miller. I'd sampled a few of the products over the years at work, but the brand took on a new meaning when Paps revealed a few of his secrets to only me.

My sister, Ashley, and I always thought he'd been in love with someone other than my grandmother, Sally, but it was only in the last few years of his life that he became more transparent. For some reason, he didn't share his story with Ashley, and I wasn't going to be the one to tell her.

Later, he admitted why he'd shared this information with me. Based on my immense loss, he wanted me to know that he too had experienced the same level of pain. The losses were not the same, but in his mind we had something in common. Mostly, I was mad at my family, the church, and our little community, all of whom had promised if I was a kind and obedient girl, good things would happen. They didn't happen.

Paps had spent a good part of his life at odds with his religion after his broken love story—maybe that was why he lumped us together. But he could've stood up and had a happier ending. I was sure of it and desperately needed to know why not.

Now, tucked in my pencil skirt and blazer, I spent most of the day dealing with men like Mack. Arrogant, wealthy, and powerful assholes, who thought they could do no wrong and deserved everyone's attention the minute they occupied a room. Well, I wasn't afraid of his kind, and

I'd strode into work armed with a fresh batch of cookies and planned to ambush the man in question at the end of the workday.

The minute I'd stormed into his office, I almost forgot my mission. That was the most terrifying problem with Mackenzie Miller—he cast a spell on me, causing me to lose my words and my way if I wasn't careful.

If he got his looks and charisma from his grandma, I understood why my Paps fell for her.

All I wanted was to show him some of the letters I'd found and apologize for any actions on the part of my family that might have led to Rose's unease. Although I suspected her family was the more outspoken one, not mine. My parents seemed to be the first generation to treat children with hostility, but that was a different story arc.

But…but…when it came to this particular tale, freaking Mack Miller got under my skin. Literally, I felt twitchy when I was around him; my fingers burned to touch and feel him all over. And then I went and held his hand and a fire erupted in my belly. I was an active volcano when it came to him, and he wasn't the least bit affected. At all. He'd dismissed me for the second time, and to say my ego was bruised was putting it lightly.

I wasn't sure if it was my need to share the information with him or his lack of sensing my feelings or both, but when I got home on Friday night I made it my personal mission to get the man to agree to meet with me.

Google was my friend. He'd mentioned golf, and that was where I started. After a quick search, the internet turned up a decade's worth of pictures of Mack at his golf club with several of his football teammates and wealthy buddies. One giant in particular, who had played professionally. Most recently, the handsome and generous Mack Miller—their words—had recently attended a fundraiser for a local women's shelter and played in a tournament benefitting the Boys and Girls Club with Ryder Fyrst and Spencer Kline.

I barely looked at the other subjects, my eyes laser focused on the source of my investigation. He was smiling in every picture, standing next to a friend or two, and never beside a woman. In one picture, Mack was standing with a cousin named Tom. And I could tell by his body language that he didn't care for this guy, but was in it for the cause. My initial research proved Mack Miller had a heart somewhere inside his tough exterior.

When I dove deeper, the articles on his business dealings said otherwise. *Miller is ruthless when it comes to his negotiations and takeovers*—again, their words—but his rating as an employer was sky-high. Everyone who worked at Silky Skin, Milly's, or the factory or offices loved their job. It was a safe environment with full benefits and a family-like atmosphere.

It was an enigma how such a staunch businessman created such a warm work environment.

I'd been on my Mack Miller internet search for more hours than I cared to admit…when Saturday afternoon I'd fallen asleep on the couch, the laptop still on my legs. I'd woken to my phone buzzing and my thighs on fire from the computer's heat.

"Hello?" My throat scratchy from sleep, I didn't bother to look at caller ID.

"Frankie? What are you doing home? It's Saturday… I sent a colleague, Matthew, in to see you."

I squeezed my eyes shut and wished I hadn't answered. "Hello, Jeremy. So nice of you to check in. I'm well, thanks."

"I'm not checking in. I sent you a client, and you're not at work on a Saturday. Isn't that the busiest day of the week for retail?"

Sitting up, I set the laptop on the coffee table and leaned back into the couch, sticking the phone on speaker. "Not that I owe you an explanation, Jer, but I don't work Saturdays anymore unless someone asks me to. I'm mostly working with my book of business and not taking new customers. It's been a long time since I've depended on weekend walk-ins. Not that you should care or it's any of your business."

I hated that his nickname came out of my mouth, a habit I'd never been able to kick. A long time ago, I'd thought Jeremy Ross was the love of my life. Yeah, he'd been captain of the football and basketball teams, and I was a cheerleader. And we all knew those relationships only worked out in the movies. But somewhere in my brain, I'd believed I was the one who would make it happen.

I was a sucker for love stories and fancied myself above a tragic breakup, until it was my reality.

"Matthew just made partner at his law firm. He really needs to up his game. A real shame you don't want to keep growing your book. Don't you think that is self-limiting? Oh, it must be the settlement you got from me?"

I felt my body shaking before I visibly saw my hands tremble. "Listen, I'm not up for this. Not now or ever. Please don't send me clients or call me. You paid me off to get out of your world and take care of a baby you didn't want. Then I lost the baby and almost died in the process. So stay out of my life. I'm living it how I want, considering I almost lost it."

I disconnected the call before he could respond. Standing up, I decided a fresh cup of coffee was needed. Then I could start figuring out how I could get through to Mack Miller.

My Paps's great love story needed to be heard and the blanks filled in.

It wasn't until later that day I saw it—*boom*. I'd been half searching while getting dressed to meet my friend Rachel for dinner, and there it was—a pot of gold at the end of my rainbow. This coming week, Silky Skin was partnering with a different department store than the one I worked for to do makeovers for women heading back to the workforce. I wasn't sure if the CEO would be there, but all I had to do was take a few hours off work and go see.

I mean, he should go. Right? It was a big publicity boon...

"*H*onestly, the guy is strange. He's all hard edges and formidable in person, but then he sponsors an event like this." I admitted more than I wanted to over a cocktail with Rachel.

"Frankie, darling, I have to be the voice of reason. This guy isn't interested in what you're peddling, and I just don't want to see you get hurt." Her hand stilled while smoothing her own black hair and she took my fingers in hers.

A laugh tumbled out of my chest, remembering how I'd done the same to Mack. "I don't like the guy, Rach. I don't even know if *like* is in my vocabulary after Jeremy. I just want to put all the pieces together of my Paps's story. And maybe Mack Miller can help me find some clues. There has to be something Rosie left behind. I could help him find it."

Rachel took a sip of her cabernet and looked at me dead-on, "Frankie, I know you. Remember, I was there when Jeremy sidelined you. I was the one who took you to the emergency room when everything went down, and you mumbled the whole time, 'Where's my happily-ever-after?' I just don't want you to think Mack is it."

Knocking back the last dregs of my scotch, I allowed it to burn my throat in the way my Paps had taught me to appreciate. Rachel had been there for me until my sister showed up and took over, and then when Ashley disappeared, my friend took over. Again. "Don't worry. I should've thought about your candor when making you my best friend. You know you can be brutal?"

Her head fell back, exposing her smooth olive skin down her neckline into the V-neck of her summer cashmere vest. "My candor? My grandma would call it chutzpah. Nerve, you know?"

I know. I remember your bubbe, Sophie, saying what chutzpah Jeremy had…"

Rachel smiled at my butchering of the *ch* sound. It was supposed to sound more raspy, less stilted than my using an *h*, leaving off the *c* all together.

"Don't get hurt, okay? Paps wouldn't want that." Rachel let it go at that.

We spent the remainder of the night having a second drink, gabbing about her blind date, and munching on a charcuterie plate.

Sunday, I woke with a resolve to think about letting the whole mission go. Maybe Rachel was right, and I was looking at Mack Miller through rose-colored sunglasses.

Until Monday, when Jeremy's friend Matthew showed up at my store, harassing me over a sale suit, and I spent every free moment daydreaming about my grandpap and some woman named Rosie. I imagined them stealing away for kisses in back alleys and him bringing her daisies the way he used to bring me. In a weird turn of events, my fantasy switched to Mackenzie Miller bringing me expensive bouquets—bright wildflowers—and leaning in to brush his lips along my cheek.

That was when I knew Rachel was absolutely correct: I was putting Mack on a pedestal. But it didn't matter because I had to figure out what happened with Paps and Milly, no matter what.

CHAPTER Four

MACK

"Are you in, or what? It's one night, maybe more…"

My best buddy, Spencer, had been on the phone, going after me for the last ten minutes over an impending double date with two supermodels from California. He was unofficially dating one of them.

"Dude," he went on like the born and bred West Coast boy he was, "I'm telling you, she's gorgeous. *Sports Illustrated* swimsuit hot. And smart! You seemed into the idea last weekend."

I'd halfheartedly agreed to the whole double date when we'd been on a golf weekend, just to get the guys off my back. *You never date,* they'd ribbed. *Just take 'em home and send them on their way. And they don't mind! Don't you want to wake up to the same gorgeous, intelligent seductress in the morning?*

This was mostly Ryan talking, but Ryder also had chimed in. *The married life isn't so bad,* he'd said unconvincingly.

I like my coffee alone in my kitchen and black like my heart. I'm glad you enjoy being married, Ry. And as for my lack of dating, it's my choice, was my response while rolling my eyes. These guys had been in my life since grad school, and while I hated to admit it, they were the closest I had to family other than Milly and one lone guy from my football days.

The coffee bit was my usual reply to this type of commentary. Ryan and Spencer were my non-football friends. Spence and I were proudly still single while Ryan was married to his college sweetheart. Ryder was on his third wife, so he surely wasn't influencing me anytime soon.

Alone and black is cold and lonely. You know what? You should pick up a romance book and see what love is all about. Plus they're hot! Trish is devouring one as we speak, and I reap the rewards, Ryan had said. He was so smitten, and it showed.

Okay Ry, I'd told him. *I'll take your word for it.* I wasn't having it.

Don't blame me. Go out with Spence's friend. Maybe you'll fall for someone for a night or three. Make it a multiple-night romp in the sheets and maybe more.

Sadly, this was the typical ribbing that went on between my graduate school guy friends and me. I held myself up as a politically correct type of man and often was annoyed with them for their crude banter. I hated locker room talk—even the idea of it, the nickname and all, perturbed me—since my junior year in college. It could have been Milly's influence, or the time I was the focus of the talk, but I shoved all that shit to the back of my mind.

Especially Milly. She was taking up ample space lately. And as for the past, I'd spent enough time dwelling on those dreadful months of college.

My graduate school friends and buddies only grasped part of my relationship history but wanted me to date regularly. They knew for certain that I had my nights in the sheets, but those weren't part of my talking points. Usually whomever I found myself in bed with understood it was simply lust or scratching an itch, and it was the same for them. Women were liberated these days and were allowed to be their own sexual beings with other priorities than landing a man.

"Come on. Melinda won't go unless I find someone for Sela," Spencer finally admitted, still droning on.

Despite his blond locks and easygoing attitude, Spencer was anything but. When he set his eyes on a prize, it usually became his. One thing though, he never accused me of being anything but myself—a loner when it came to love. His brother was gay, and he too led the charge in dispelling myths when it came to relationships with our asshole friends. But this time felt different. And I might be a solo man when it came to everlasting shit, but I was a damn good friend.

"I really like Melinda and want to see her again, and this is the situation. So do me a solid. Okay, man?"

"Okay, I'll go, but I have to make an appearance at a work event first in Herald Square. Then I can swing over to the Athletic Club. Is that where you're meeting?"

"I would never want to disappoint Melinda. Never."

"I know, I know. Now shut it and let me get back to work."

Spencer disconnected the call, knowing I'd be there to chat up sensual Sela while he tried to sell himself further to Melinda, the supermodel. It wasn't a punishment. Plus I had to respect a woman who wouldn't ditch her friend, and a man who would do anything to make a woman happy.

I knew nothing about either.

"Ready?" Corey popped his head in my office a few hours later.

I was getting off a conference call with the managers of Silky, discussing a new rollout of scented lotions. I nodded, taking one last look at my emails and standing up. "Give me a minute to change into a fresh shirt."

"Got it," Corey said, heading back out to his desk.

Stepping into my private bathroom, I wondered why I had agreed to this event, let alone the date. Because I wasn't an evil man. I cared for my friends and the community, or so I told myself.

I was wondering if anyone else recognized this about me when Corey said, "Thanks again." He spoke quickly as I came strolling out of my office in a white shirt and the same dark gray pants I'd been wearing. I'd traded my Ferragamos for black-on-black Gucci sneakers, and swapped belts.

"No worries," I told Corey for what felt like the eighteenth time, but maybe it was the first. I was beginning to wonder...

"Bailey is super appreciative," Corey added.

With a nod, I dismissed the conversation, but I could tell Corey was still mulling over my involvement in the *Back to Work, Ladies* event. "It's a win-win. Bailey knocked it out of the park in her job, bringing in a company like Silky to partner. And we look like heroes. I like your sister and all, but I don't do anything that doesn't benefit me. Stop worrying yourself over it."

To this, Corey laughed.

We slid into the SUV Alex kept idling for us and headed to Midtown.

"I am heading to the Athletic Club after, and then you can drop Corey wherever he is going," I told Alex before opening my phone and checking a few stocks.

"The bergamot is expected to ship tomorrow, so the factory will have it in two days," Corey told me, and I looked up.

"Good. From what I understand, Milly's signature scent is almost sold out in most stores."

"Yeah. Apparently, it's an expected add-on when making a purchase."

"That's what I like to hear, Corey. I need to promote you, but then who will put up with my shit?"

Corey wasn't just any assistant. He spoke with everyone from store managers to vendors; he knew the pulse on the overall market and our business's performance.

"I like where I am, but I wouldn't say no to a raise..."

I howled. "You know all you have to do is ask. But you shouldn't be so comfortable in your place. You're smart. You could get an MBA and move up in the company."

Corey suffered from small-town phobia. He grew up on a farm in central Pennsylvania. He was the only gay guy he knew until his sophomore year of college. He'd told me all this over a scotch one evening. He'd only dated a little at a small business college outside Erie, Pennsylvania. I joked with him that the idea of it made me sick. Not only dating a little, but rural USA wasn't my scene.

"Who would manage you and run interference with your recent stalker, then?" He smiled at me, waiting for me to deny I had a situation with Frances Burns.

"I'm sure anyone could handle me. The feisty blond bombshell, I'm not so certain. She does a damn good job of working her way around you."

"You like her." His mouth twisted upward in a smirk.

"I found her amusing," was all I admitted. "Back to you and the MBA. What do you say? Maybe some night classes at CUNY? Or I could call in a favor at Fordham?"

He turned his gaze away from mine. "I don't know. I went to Podunk College and got a degree in business administration. I hardly think I'm CEO material."

"Who said anything about CEO? Are you taking my job already?" This had us both laughing again, and I made a mental note to call around on Corey getting an MBA as we slid up in front of one of New York's most famous landmark department stores.

Inhaling and exhaling, I got out of the car before Alex could open the door. The sooner I showed my face at the event, the faster I could get to my non-date and then home. For a flash, I thought about starting to drive myself again, and then let the idea go. It had been a long time since I'd sold the Porsche my dad had given me in college for a down payment on a condo. My dad made up for his emotional absence with being financially generous. I would have preferred him to work on improving the former, but he had been gone for a while, and I'd learned there was no correcting the past.

Lost in my sappy thoughts, I was walking around, showing my face and shaking hands with a few society women, when I spotted her. She was standing by the last station where women were taking pictures in front of a big green screen. It was a headshot booth where they snapped interview-ready photos. I'd loved the idea when I read about it. But seeing Frances Burns cheering these ladies on made me feel other sorts of ways. Unsure, mostly.

Did she genuinely think this was a good idea? Why was she here, when she worked at a different department store? My brain went into overdrive the way it always did around the woman. She couldn't weigh more than a hundred and ten pounds, yet her presence was like a giant elephant walking the streets of New York.

Not that I would ever say that to her. One, you never spoke about a woman's weight. Milly taught me that. And two, I wasn't sure an elephant was the type of comparison any person wanted to hear about themselves.

I took her in—Frances smiled like a goofball at every one—and I wasn't a lip-reader, but it seemed like she complimented each woman.

Unable to resist, I sidled up next to her, whispering for her ears only. "If I didn't know better, I might suggest you found me here on purpose, Ms. Burns. But that's not the type of woman you are, is it? Let's see, persistent, dogged, and more determined than anyone I know? *That's not you.* You must believe in serendipity. Or are you someone who must get their way, no matter what?"

Thinking back to my grandmother, Frankie had better be in the latter group and not one into gratuitous meetings... I'd prefer a stalker.

"Why hello, Mr. Miller. Fancy seeing you here." She made an *O* with her mouth, feigning shock.

"Oh, you mean you didn't notice my company's name on every

sign for the event? You may need glasses, Frances."

This earned me a chuckle, and if I was interested in honesty, I'd say how much I loved hearing the sound. But when it came to Frances Burns, honesty wasn't going to serve me well.

Turning to face me, she spoke. "You got me. I was looking for you, and then poof, there you were—at an event near and dear to my heart."

Running a hand through my hair, I wished my fingers were tangled in her long waves instead. "I thought you sold men's clothes?"

Moving a finger back and forth in front of me she tsked. "Checking on me?"

With an eyebrow raised I reminded her, "You gave me your card."

Her finger no longer wagging, she waved her hand. "Never mind. Here you are, and I'm so happy to see you. You know, this is how I found my way. It was my senior year of college and I had zero career ambitions or job prospects. I went to a women's gathering out on Long Island, and rather than allow them to fix me up, I charged in and started assisting everyone else."

"Why doesn't that surprise me?"

"Right? I discovered that I enjoyed getting everyone ready for war. Fashion, retail, and customer service was my calling."

Either she refused to hear my sarcasm or she genuinely thought I was impressed. Well, I was, but I wasn't sure I should let her in on it. "That's incredible," I finally said and meant it—yet the idea scared me. "Are you looking to change it up? Women instead of men?" There was a tinge of bite in my words, and I watched Frankie frown. "I'm sorry, that wasn't kind. It was more for me than you. We keep running into one another, and I'd be lying if I said it wasn't affecting me." It was all I gave up, but more truth than I wanted to admit.

"Great! Maybe we can grab dinner afterward? You can tell me about the ins and outs of the event. I'd like to host one for men." Full-on grinning again, Feisty Frankie didn't miss a beat. If there was a tiny crack to crawl in, she got down on all fours and found her way.

"You should talk to Corey—you've already met him several times. His sister works for the agency co-sponsoring this event. He would better know the information you need."

I followed her tongue licking over her bottom lip…

"So, this had nothing to do with your benevolence? This event?" Her small fingers waved around the giant floor of the department store. In a swirl of wildly dressed people, Ed Sheeran crooning, a host of perfume smells and bright colors, all I saw were her pale pink manicured nails.

More fissures. The longer I spent in Frankie's company, the greater chance I had of being cracked wide open.

Not to mention, right about now my thoughts were far from benevolent…

Pulling my mind out of the gutter, I cleared the tickle in my throat. "What can I do for you, Frances? And no, this wasn't kindhearted or socially motivated, it was a business move on my part. I have a business side and a personal side. If we were close, you would know this about me. You would also know my personal side is extremely limited. But we're not remotely close," I parroted myself. "You keep trying to ask me for favors of a personal nature while I'm in work mode. If I was in the mood to help you, which I'm not, I'd suggest you find a different way to reach me."

She didn't answer but started rummaging through the ginormous cream-colored tote hanging from her shoulder. Extracting her phone, she said, "Okay, so lunch on a weekend? That works."

I couldn't help the laugh rumbling from my chest. "You have no shame."

My six-foot-three frame towered over the five-foot-and-change Frances Burns, and yet, she acted as if she was a seven-foot former NBA player, current Wall Street tycoon, and I was subservient to her.

"I don't, by the way." She answered my question. "I think you called me dogged. It was meant to be an insult, but I took it as a compliment.

I've supported myself, built a career, and now found you…several times. The least you could do is have lunch. Look at my Paps's journal. Maybe rifle through some of Rosie's—I mean Milly's old belongings. I bet you still have everything in that musty old house in Westchester she lived in…"

My gaze scanned the area. "Do you have eyes on me?" This woman knew almost everything about me. It should scare me; Corey might have been right. I had a stalker.

"No! I'm not that kind of person. Your bio is available everywhere…I mean, except the tidbits on your mom. And I would never share those. But it's not hard to figure out. You grew up with your grandmother in Westchester. I didn't see any sale of the house when searching for Rosie, so I assumed. But again, I would never, ever share the information about your mom. That's personal." Poor Frances was flustered and rambled on.

"I'm not sure *never* is in your vocabulary."

A small frown flashed across her face. She quickly schooled the look, but I didn't like what it might mean. Which for the record, I had no clue, but the thought of this cannonball of a woman thinking anything might never be in her grasp hurt me.

Not to mention something I said made her sad.

This was precisely what I meant when I said there was a business part of me and my personal life was separate. I didn't like mixing the two because emotions didn't have a seat in the boardroom.

"It is, believe me." The small scowl made another short appearance in her admission, and then it was gone. "Let's make a lunch plan, or even dinner now…"

"I'll tell you this—I will agree to lunch. On a weekend. Call Corey in the morning to schedule, and I'll be sure to let him know to get it done. I'm sorry, Frankie, but right now I have a date." Unsure why I agreed to a meeting with her, I got the final word.

Catching a quick look at Frances Burns and her reddening cheeks before scurrying out had me feeling more unsettled than I had in years. I didn't like it; my mom made me feel like my emotions were being picked apart and I'd done my best to let that feeling be.

Though, I had to say, my mentioning a date and Frankie's reaction did something to me—and much later, it wasn't the boring evening spent with Sela guiding my hand. It was Frankie's image burned on my brain, her dry wit and sweet side and balls-to-the-wall personality rattling in the brain.

I had to exorcise the woman from my system.

CHAPTER *Five*

FRANKIE

"That prick!" I stomped my foot when I got home. "A date!" I screamed at myself in the mirror.

I brushed my teeth with reckless abandon. My poor skin had never been more raw or cleaner after a brutal scrubbing.

Shoving my legs into my Garfield pajama pants, I scurried out to my kitchen for a pint of ice cream.

"Jerk," I declared, opening a brand spanking new tub of peppermint bark ice cream. I bought out all the leftover stock after Christmas every damn year. Sadly, it was a seasonal offering, and currently it was the only treat I bothered carrying up to my apartment, and the solo occupant of my freezer other than a bottle of vodka.

Plopping on the couch, I let the pale pink, cool, and minty mixture tickle my throat. I savored each tiny piece of candy cane and morsel of dark chocolate. My stomach would be bloated all the way to work in the morning, but this very moment was worth it. And needed.

Sad but true: peppermint bark ice cream was my greatest

indulgence.

I made a mental note not to look at myself in the mirror and to walk to work from my place rather than Uber or subway, allowing the movement to deflate my belly.

Leaning my head back, I breathed in and out, trying to stop my mind from imagining Mackenzie Dickish Miller on his date. I bet she was tall and lean…and young and fertile.

But why did I care? He was nothing more than a missing piece to a puzzle I wanted to solve.

How dare he blow me off again. Okay, we didn't have a firm plan or any arrangements at all. He hadn't known I would be at the event, and I shouldn't have expected him to agree to my terms—he'd said no already twice.

But third time's a charm, right?

I continued to devour my ice cream, snatching the remote from the coffee table and wondering what Miller's date was eating. Probably a salad. Why did this all bother me so much? I'd relegated myself to a lonely life, busy with work and friends.

This mystery woman—*the dick's date*—likely hadn't miscarried a baby at twenty-five weeks, leaving her to deliver a stillborn and work for a year and a half to take the baby weight off, but that wasn't the point. This was my world, and I was living in it. Many of the choices had been my own. Yeah, I didn't bargain on losing the baby, but I had married Jeremy. Willingly.

Hitting the button for Christmas Romances on Netflix, I became even firmer in my decision to investigate Paps's great love story. If I couldn't have my own beautiful story, I'd settle for year-round holiday-infused romance movies and my grandpa's love affair instead. Dipping my spoon into my ice cream again, I let all the negative thoughts go and focused on what time of day I should call Corey tomorrow. I had a lull in my appointments around two and decided it was the perfect time. Not too early or too late.

"*I* know exactly who you are," Corey said over the phone after I introduced myself. "And you have some mighty big balls. Pardon me for saying it, but you do."

I couldn't help the giggle before clearing my throat and stating, "I'm pretty sure that's not appropriate for you to say over the phone to a woman."

"Oh, I know. But at this point I'd even take you suing me to get more interactions between you and the boss. There is no better entertainment. I mean, what are you? Four-eleven?"

"Five foot one," I answered proudly.

"Okay, we'll say five feet, and you take on that big brute, no matter the issue. You know he's practically a hermit? Do you? Yet you come barging in any time of day, shoving baked goods at security, making Millsy squirm. I love it. I downright love it."

"Millsy?" I felt like I'd just been gifted a pint of ice cream, but I'd have to wait to eat it because I was bloated like a whale from the night before. "I'll hold on to that teensy nugget," I told Corey, and I would. I'd keep Millsy in my back pocket for when I needed it. Until then, I'd finish the task at hand.

"Don't think mentioning it to Miller will change a thing. He knows the office refers to him as Millsy, laughs every time he walks in on a conversation where he thinks it might have been used. He's not penetrable. That's what you don't get. Guy is steel when it comes to getting in deep."

"About the reason for this call. Mr. Miller said to give you a ring and set up a lunch appointment. I guess I am getting through…"

"Sure. He said to make it soon. A little thing about 'getting it over with' but I'm thrilled you're getting through."

I leaned into the counter in my personal office—the ladies' room. I never understood why they placed it behind the men's section, but it suited me. "Are you having fun at my expense? We have really gone three-sixty in this call. First, you commend me about my balls, claiming you can't get enough of me and your boss. And now…you are insulting me?"

"Not insulting. More warning." He took on a deep tone. "Mack is a good guy, loved by everyone here. He doesn't have many who care for him, and he is opening up to you. Yeah, he may want to get it over quickly, but you seem to have a lasting effect on him."

"I am not the enemy. I'm just a woman who needs help learning about Rose Miller."

"Hmmm," Corey hummed. It felt like Mack hadn't clued him in to our business.

"I'm doing some research on her. That's all."

"Hmmm," again from the other side of the line.

"So, lunch?" I brought us back on track.

"How's Saturday?"

"You mean tomorrow?"

"You're quick. Yeah, tomorrow. Mack can meet you at one o'clock."

"Of course, great, thank you."

He rattled off an intersection and added, "It's in the Meatpacking. Don't be late."

I knew where he meant—it was a member's-only spot for the creative world. A safe, chic, and beautiful haven in the middle of a concrete jungle. "I won't," I assured Corey.

He disconnected the call, and I went to pee, wondering while crouching over the toilet if this was a true olive branch or a pity lunch.

*A*rmed in a white summer cashmere sweater and linen pants, I stepped inside Mack's club at five minutes to one on Saturday. I'd been to the elusive venue a few times before…when I was still with Jeremy. I'd made a habit of not returning until now. But who was I to argue with Corey?

"Can I help you?" the skinny woman in all black asked me from behind the front desk.

The club was for wealthy creatives—movers and shakers in the arts, music, and things like advertising and public relations—so I couldn't help but wonder why Mack went there.

"Frankie Burns. I'm meeting Mackenzie Miller." I took in her muscular arms on display and the black lacy tank covering her flat chest. I was sure she didn't have a belly like mine. Or an ass, but none of this mattered.

"Oh, you mean Mack?"

Of course she called him Mack. Most CEOs would expect to be referred to as Mr. So-and-So, but not Mackenzie Miller. He exuded an air of confidence and power coupled with a casual nature…with everyone but me.

"Yes, Mack," I confirmed.

"He's on the rooftop, by the pool. Can I see your ID and then you can head up."

I swiped my wallet out of my tote, snagging my license from the side, and handed it over.

This place was such a sideshow in and of itself. It was just lunch. I wasn't going to steal anything or take anyone's photo. I knew that to be a rule—no photos in the club.

She perused my information and handed me back my license and waved me on like the insignificant person I was.

In the elevator, I reprimanded myself for my outfit. Who knew he would pick outside to eat? Not me. I imagined Mack spent his weekend in a suit, and I was way off base when I stepped off the elevator and found him waiting directly outside the doors in khaki pants and a polo.

"Frances." That was how he greeted me, low and laced with a masculinity I couldn't quite describe.

"Mack," I served back. "Thanks for agreeing to meet me," I offered.

"It's my pleasure," he lobbed.

"Shall we?" He motioned toward the bar and a few tables speckled around it.

"We shall."

We continued to spar with words as he pulled out my seat.

"Hope this is okay," he said, looking my white outfit up and down.

"Why wouldn't it be?"

"You're…a little dressed up. Are you supposed to be showing your angelic side? Did you think this was a date?" He slid across from me, the sun plinking off his dirty-brown hair. I hadn't noticed before, but Mack Miller didn't look Jewish… It wasn't a kind thing to think, and I centered my thoughts. I wasn't that person. Jewish didn't have a look…

"I'm hardly an angel, but I don't date men who went out two nights prior on a different date."

"You like a fairy tale, don't you?" His left eyebrow rose as he asked, and I felt the urge to flight or fight.

I looked away. All of a sudden, I wasn't sure if I could do this.

"I'm sorry. We're all entitled to like what we want. Sometimes my cynicism ruins everything."

It was the most honest moment we'd shared. Turning back toward Mack, my gaze caught his gray eyes, a tad softer, almost somber. "If you must know, I do believe in fairy tales…and nightmares…and something mediocre in between. You know, like enough, but not really? My Paps lived in the in-between, in the gray area where he was happy but not ecstatic. But he dreamed about what it would have been like with his Rosie. I bet it would have been multicolor and glittery and more than a fairy tale."

"It never is really all that." He contradicted my sentiment. "My grandmother is Rosie in this scenario. At least, you suspect?" Mack looked at me, raising an eyebrow.

"Yes. I know Rosie is your grandma. He'd mention her from time to time when we were teenagers. And then in his final years he spoke about *Rosie* a lot. For my own peace of mind, I just want to know their story. Maybe it would explain the low level of sadness always lingering on him."

Mack had leaned forward to speak when a server swung by asking if we wanted a drink.

Mack looked to me, and I spoke up, needing a bit more courage. "White wine, something dry. I'm not picky."

The server nodded.

"Bloody Mary," came from the man across from me. It was an interesting choice. "They do a prix fixe brunch, is that okay with you? I went ahead and requested it for us."

I could've argued, but a gentle nod came from me.

While a basket of muffins and pastries arrived, followed by our cocktails, I spotted a few other tables occupied by city dwellers who hadn't escaped to the Hamptons, enjoying their weekend, sipping drinks and eating eggs.

"What about the sadness you carry?"

"I'm sorry?" My hand shook, forcing me to set my wineglass back down.

"You. I can't help but notice there is a current of unease—of hurt, or pain—that flashes off you every so often. Yeah, you're funny, and your words can bite, and you kickbox, but you're also sad. What happened, Frances?"

He ran a hand through his hair, his bulky gold watch catching the light.

"This isn't about me."

"Do you want to find out about Rosie, who let's refer to as Milly from here on out?"

"I do."

"Then that's the price. I answer what you ask, and you tell me what I want to know."

"Why? W-why do you want to know about me?" I stuttered over my words.

I watched him swallow, a lump passing over his Adam's apple, and waited. This man ran a multimillion-dollar empire. And yeah, I'd harassed him to meet with me, but not to inquire as to my feelings. Yes, he was sexy and exuded some sort of hormone that made me want to run my fingers over his skin, but that wasn't the point.

"I don't know why, but I do."

Again, more honesty. It was such a contradiction to the man's position and authority.

A server interrupted again, this time with frittatas and toast and some sort of arugula salad.

I stuck my fork into the greens and then stopped. Mack's heated gaze was on me; he was waiting for an answer.

"I was hurt," I said. "I thought I'd found my fairy tale, but it turned out to be more than a nightmare. Now, I work and enjoy time with friends, but I don't believe in that sort of happily-ever-after for myself anymore." Without waiting, I stuffed my mouth with lemon-dressed arugula so I wouldn't say any more. Next thing, I'd spill my guts and talk about the stillbirth and start crying.

"So, you're going to live vicariously through your grandpa's past? Is that it?"

"Bingo!"

"Tell me about the kickboxing." That's what he said before taking a bite of his frittata, skipping the arugula.

I laughed. "Seriously?"

"Seriously. We'll come back to all that pain and suffering later. Besides, I know what you do for work. And I buy custom-made suits, so it's a bad subject for us."

Guzzling a little wine, I let the alcohol tingle my throat. "I like it. Kickboxing. It feels liberating. A time when we can be aggressive and express ourselves…"

"Hmmm. I get it. I used to feel that way in college sports. It's probably why Milly enrolled me in soccer as a kid. It was a way to take out the anger, be competitive, and earn my own…I don't know what.

Pride, perhaps."

I didn't want to admit it, but I liked his sincerity. Most people I met these days were not honest and real. "Yes, it's about me, accomplishing something no one believed I could," I admitted.

"Exactly. There is something thrilling about doing what everyone said you couldn't…"

He said it with the corner of his mouth tipped up, and I couldn't help but ask, "What are you thinking?"

"I'm thinking about doing something on my own. Like when I travel, and I sit on the balcony in boxer shorts and drink a coffee without anyone pestering me. Although I feel like you'd find me."

"Ha, ha! Probably, if you hadn't agreed to meet me. Tell me, when can we talk about Ros—Milly?"

He smiled, his white teeth on display. "Next time we get together."

"Next time?"

"Yeah. Now we're going to order another drink and unpack all this misery you're toting around."

"Ummm…"

"I can't believe it—I've rendered all four-feet-and-change of Feisty Frankie wordless. Don't kickbox me out of here."

If I wasn't in all white and gladiator sandals, I might have…

MACK

Tuesday, I heard the weight bar clang as I racked it before snagging a towel to wipe the sweat off my shoulder.

"You have two more," Neil, my expensive-as-hell trainer said matter-of-factly.

"Take it easy…I'll get to them…I'm paying you."

It was a near constant joke between the two of us. He pushed me and I complained every step of the way, wondering why I hired him to do this to me.

"What's up with you today? You still mad about the date? Poor baby, I forced you to meet a supermodel."

I looked over at Spencer doing squats in the mirror.

"You know this is my gym, right? Anyway, that fiasco? It was last week. I've forgotten about it already."

He laughed, setting down the dumbbell he'd been holding.

"Let's go," Neil barked then ribbed us some more. "If you ladies wanted to chat, you should've gone for coffee."

I hoisted the bar off the rack and started with my deadlifts.

"Good for your running, boss. Keep it up," Neil said to me before instructing Spencer to do push-ups.

"Now Millsy, what's eating you?" Spencer spoke through broken breaths.

Fucking Corey had called me Millsy once in front of Spencer, and now he picked only the most special times to bring it out.

Racking the bar early again, I blew out a breath.

This whole scenario reminded me of a different time and place in a weight room. Of course, one woman had changed—the love interest—and the other hadn't.

"Women problems?" Neil asked, an eyebrow raised. "Aren't you a little too old for that?"

"I don't pay you to be my therapist, and just because I have a decade on you doesn't mean I'm old."

More whispers of the past. My teammate, Teddy, had tried to help, and I'd accused him of being a shrink. Insulted him along the way too.

Neil leaned into the mirrored wall. I'd turned my third bedroom into an exercise room. Bachelor's prerogative, I called it. It was meant to be a nursery, but there would be none of that around here...

"Spill it." Spencer stared me down, now on his back on the mat.

"Apparently my grandmother is coming back to haunt me."

"Not what I expected to hear," came from Spence on a long breath. "Interesting, I'll admit, but not your everyday kind of guy talk."

"I didn't take you as the kind to believe in ghosts," came from Neil. "Give me some crunches," he added, looking at me, and I dropped to a mat on the other side of Spencer.

Through gritted teeth, I spoke. "Not her actual ghost. Her past. There's some girl...woman...who claims her grandpa was the long-lost love of my grandmother's. I don't know if it's true or what happened or why she even cares, but uncovering their story is her current life mission. And I'm her accomplice whether I want to be or not."

"Tell me this, is she smoking hot? Enough for you to turn down going home with Sela? Is that what happened last week? I didn't know you were interested in someone else, or I wouldn't have pushed the agenda."

"Dude…what are you, twenty-five? Smoking hot?"

"Says the guy saying 'dude.'"

I couldn't help a belly laugh escaping me. "Ouch," I said, holding my core.

Neil recentered us. "So what's the issue? Spit it out and we can get back to your workout."

"This woman has literally hunted me down and trapped me in this romantic mission with her."

"Pretty sure no one traps you in anything, Millsy. Now I know she's gotta be hot and smart and interesting and worth it." Spencer stood and grabbed a water bottle.

Getting up myself, I turned to face my friend. "I appreciate all your rambling on and on. Yes, she is extremely attractive, curvy, younger, huge green eyes, smart with a knack for little zings, and wounded…in a way that compels me. That's the problem. And now I'm tasked with helping her research my family, which is the last fucking thing I want to do. Yet I agreed to all of the above."

"Back to bicep curls because you need a therapist for this," Neil directed.

"You do, man. You really fucking do. It's like your worst nightmare wrapped up in one. A broken, gorgeous woman and your shitty family history. All your kryptonites. Is she trying to bandage your abandonment issues too?"

I nodded, lugging the thirties and starting to curl. "You know she is…they all want to make up for my lack of a mother."

As I said it, I knew these two were right; I needed therapy.

Instead, I found myself meeting Frankie at her kickboxing class on Wednesday. If the guys only knew I was group kickboxing… I could practically hear them laughing like hyenas.

"Hope you can keep up with me," she said outside the boutique fitness studio before yanking the door open.

She was still in her work clothes—shiny, pale pink Mary Janes on her feet, silver-gray pencil skirt, an ivory sleeveless blouse, and a huge sparkly tote slung over her shoulder. Took me all of three seconds to catalog every inch of her like a desperate and thirsty man searching for water and she was a bubbling stream.

We signed in at the desk, Frances quickly letting them know she'd booked both of us on her package.

"Dinner is on me." I said it without us even discussing grabbing a meal after, but the evening already felt too short. For someone who didn't enjoy spending time with many people, being with Frances felt inviting, natural, and like it was never enough.

"I need a minute to change." She ignored my offer, looking me up and down, taking in my track pants and jacket.

"I'll just leave this in a locker." Waving a hand in front of my body, I'd never felt more at a loss for something to say.

How was it this small creature unraveled me?

"Meet you back here," she stated and sauntered off.

If it took me three seconds to note her work outfit, it took less to take in her workout wear. Black biker shorts, a strappy red tank thing, and her hair tied tight in a ponytail, sneakers on her feet.

"Ready?"

I nodded.

What happened next was a blur. Some hunk named Roy led us through a warm-up, notably passing behind Frances every time we hit down dog. Next, he worked us through our uppercuts and a bunch of other jabs and crosses, which only left me wanting to jab him every time he adjusted Frances's form.

Sweat beaded on my back as we filtered in front of our punching bags and started the routine. Frankie was composed and chill as she kicked the bag, raising her leg and whipping it through the air. Her hair bounced in the process, allowing her scent to waft my way. *Milly's...* I noted.

"Having fun?"

Her words were meant for me, but Roy noted our conversation and took the class up a notch. Falling in line with his sequence of jabs and kicks, there was no way that ass was going to get the better of me.

Of course, I'd need some ibuprofen in the morning.

With a wink, I went back to work on my bag until the very end of class when I said, "I won't ever doubt you can't look out for yourself again," to Frances. When her head tilted back, a soft giggle escaped her vocal cords. My choice of stripping down to my athletic shorts was clearly a mistake. They did little to cover up my body's reaction to the supple skin leading from her collarbone to the top of her tank.

"You hung in there, tough guy," she sort of complimented me. She followed it up with, "Thanks, Roy," and of course the asshole winked and flexed his bicep before waving.

"I'm not that old, you know?" No clue as to why I confessed feeling ancient next to Roy or even Frances, but it rewarded me with another neck drop and a view at an expanse of skin I wanted to run my tongue along.

"So, dinner? And we can talk Milly?" She pulled her hair loose, allowing it to flow over her shoulders, shaking it out.

A strong desire to grab her—gently—and pull her in for a kiss took me over, and I had to shove this nonsense down. "Yeah," I agreed. "I need to grab something to wear...from my office."

We were in Chelsea, which was about twelve blocks from my offices in Hudson Yards.

"Okay," she readily agreed. "I can change, and we can go? Or should I meet you there?"

"I'll wait, take your time..."

Surprisingly, she didn't take long. I'd just finished a bottle of electrolyte water from the studio's smoothie bar when she came out of the locker room in her street clothes, smelling like eucalyptus-scented soap with a dash of Milly's perfume.

"All set?"

She nodded and we made our way out of the small storefront without seeing Roy again. *Thankfully.*

"No car?" Frances eyed me up outside as if this was a test.

"I walked."

She nodded, noting I'd passed her first quiz. Then fired off another question. "Either you don't get chauffeured everywhere or you didn't want to tell anyone where you were going..." Her hip hiked, head cocked, she watched my every move on the sidewalk.

I felt the sides of my mouth turn up. She had such nerve or chutzpah...

"What?"

I debated lying or saying nothing as we started to walk. "At least I don't have to tell you where to go. You've bombarded my office enough times."

"Very funny," she replied, turning and winking. "I'm sneaky like that. Now tell me what had you cracking a smile-slash-smirk."

"Are you sure you're not really a spy?"

"Simply smart and astute."

"And cocky?"

"Are you trying to avoid my question?"

"Milly," I admitted. "I thought about Milly, who you are only dying to discuss, and how she would say you had chutzpah."

"Hutzpah! My friend, Rachel, said the same..."

Of course she had a hard time getting out the *ch* sound. "Chutzpah," I corrected. "In the back of your throat, feel the rumble of the sound."

She gave it a few tries and ended up saying, "I know, I can't do it. Just get on with it."

We walked side by side, the heat of the day lingering on the sidewalk.

It wasn't far to Tenth and Thirtieth, and time was ticking by quickly. Maybe we'd get distracted from the question? But I quickly realized there was no deterring this woman. "It means something like bravado. You're not afraid to say what you want or mean. Milly always meant it as a good thing. In fact," I felt my voice lower at this admission, "she often said she wished she had more chutzpah when she was younger."

"Maybe she meant in regard to Paps?"

"Honestly, I have no clue. I'd never heard of James before you, so it could be. Mostly, it was when I played sports. 'Don't be shy, Mackenzie. Play hard and be brave.' When I got to college, she said, 'Make friends and do what's right.'"

"Do you have someone you can ask?"

"About what?"

"My Paps."

We were one block from my building, and I was starting to resent the project. I'd spent the better part of the last two decades shoving my family to the back of my mind. "Other than my dad's sister, no. And she's the last person on earth I want to engage. And that is a very long list she's heading up."

Another small laugh awarded me a slight view of her neck, and again the expanse I wanted to traverse. "Not even for me?"

I yanked open the door of the tower that housed my offices, and nodded to the security man as she said it.

"Hi, Miss," the detail said to Frances, confirming I was in trouble.

Not even for me?

That was the problem. For her, I'd do it, and I didn't just do stuff for most people.

"Where were your offices before?" Frances tactfully changed the subject in the elevator, and I felt a sigh of relief roll up my chest.

"Over in Midtown, but I got a tip on this area and haven't regretted it."

"No doubt. It's pretty much the hottest area in the city."

There was something about this woman. Tiny in stature, fierce in personality. Sweet in nature, sexy in every sense. Comforting when she smiled, scary when you could see her brain twitching.

"Give me a sec," I told her more for my benefit than hers. I needed a minute or ten to collect myself. I guided her to a waiting area and said, "There's water, sodas, wine, over there...I'll be right out."

I needed to grab a quick shower and change, but mostly put my armor back on before we went to the damn dinner I'd suggested. It all felt like too much and way too little at the same time; I didn't do activities coupled with dinner dates. Except, here I was.

CHAPTER Seven

FRANKIE

We went to a Mediterranean place near Hudson Yards. Of course it was hip and popular, loud and frenetic, and felt like the distraction Mack seemed to always seek. After what I'd classify as a few run-ins with the man, I already knew he evaded feelings like the plague.

Now, he sat across from me, showered and back in his suit. Literally and figuratively—he'd cloaked himself back in his emotional armor.

We ordered drinks and Mack asked the server, Luke, to bring a platter of dips while we continued our small talk. He called Luke by his first name, making eye contact, and acting as if they were old friends. I realized this was part of the reason why he was so successful: he could turn on the charm better than most and make it feel realer than anyone. Also, money and connections helped.

"An old friend of mine got heavily invested in Hudson Yards, and he suggested I take my offices there," Mack explained. Like most of his reasoning, it felt bleached of emotion, except he added a personal tidbit. "My dad would have hated it here, so I knew it was a good move. He was risk averse, and I'm not."

With my wine and his scotch, neat, in front of us, I asked, "Why do you think you're so accepting of risk?"

He smirked. "You don't know already? You didn't read it somewhere on the interwebs?"

"No, should I have seen it somewhere?"

He took a slug of his drink, and I watched his muscles work as the liquid traversed his throat, rippling over his Adam's apple. My fingers twitched to touch him, feel his pulse, bring his humanity to the surface.

"I just thought it was obvious to anyone who studied me, like you did. I have no ties to anyone, no real responsibility other than to the health of the company, so I make aggressive moves. Maybe they're bold or risky, but this business is my legacy and I can chance it."

"Is that what Milly wanted? You to chance life?" I couldn't help myself, and judging by the stare coming from Mack, he knew I couldn't resist.

He took a carrot and dipped it into hummus, stalling, crunching, and eyeing me.

I did the same.

"Is it?" I kept at it.

"No. Milly wanted a love story for me. A big Disney-worthy saga for generations to tell."

"The type of story she didn't have for herself?" My heart pounded in my chest. I wasn't sure why, but Paps's life called to me. The what-ifs and could-have-beens.

"Like I said, I don't know. Do those kinds of stories even exist other than in our imagination?" He ran a palm through his hair, his giant watch glinting in the light.

"They do," I said with determination.

Despite the small wrinkles in the corners of his eyes, he looked like a little boy who'd been told Santa wasn't real. It wasn't often optimism led to such defeat in someone's expression.

"For some people," I clarified matter-of-factly. "Not for Milly or my Paps...or—" I almost added *me*, but he interrupted me.

"My parents," he said cautiously, avoiding my gaze. With another pull on his drink, he cleared his throat. "Shit, I didn't mean to get this deep or dark. My parents' history is a tale meant to stay in the past, untold and not repeated."

"Maybe Milly and my Paps had a small period of happiness. A sliver. I guess that's why I'm so eager to understand what happened. Why did they give it up?"

"What about you? What about your happiness?" He parroted my word back to me, deflecting off himself and his grandmother.

Luke interrupted the moment. "Can I get you anything else?"

Thank God.

"Frances?" Mack looked at me.

"Um, sure. I'll have the fatoosh salad, thank you," I mumbled, almost forgetting to make eye contact with the server, quickly catching myself. Mack had knocked the bravado out of me with his question, and I was hoping he forgot the conversation after ordering.

"Any interest in fried chicken for two?"

Another punch to the gut. Fried foods only made my stomach bloated and that never boded well for my mental state.

"A bite or three?" Mack asked, driving me out of my deep thoughts.

"Sure," I found myself agreeing. "I didn't take you for a fried chicken guy," I spit out when Luke left us alone.

"Milly was the queen of comfort foods...there was a recipe for every problem. She believed in eating at home, and all this eating out we do was bad. But since I don't cook, she's made my personal trainer a very wealthy man. I eat and he does damage control."

"Hmmm, my Paps loved to eat home-cooked food. He always talked about never finding a soup quite like one he had growing up... I wonder if it was something to do with Rosie."

"Milly, you mean. We agreed." His voice was terse and tense.

I didn't know what set him off, other than guilt over fried foods. Despite his sharp tone, a quick flash of something else crossed over Mack's face, and I made a mental note to mention the home cooking at a later date.

"Back to you. Tell me about your own proposed happiness after you find out about your grandpa…" He plucked another carrot, this time dipping it in tahini, while waiting.

My throat burned with the truth… "That is my happiness. Finding out about him. That's all I want."

Mack leaned back in his chair. "Can't be. That was his life. What about yours? Certainly you want to do your own living?" His face was now gentle, a soft gaze and relaxed cheekbones. The guy was a myriad of people—stern, authoritative, kind, soulful.

"I love my work." With my statement out there, I gulped my wine.

"I'm sure you're very good at it. Thorough, smart, flirty with an eye for detail. But work isn't enough."

"Seems like it's enough for you though? And flirty? I'll have you know I'm the ultimate professional." Finally, my cynicism returned.

"Ha!" He moved forward again. "As for me, I have fun. Don't you worry, Feisty Frances, but longtime love isn't my thing. And I believe you have built a book of business based on your sheer doggedness in doing it. Nothing sinister." This came with a wink and a finger in the air, signaling for me to wait a second. "But you, my newfound friend, are a happily-ever-after girl whether you admit it or not. You believe there is a knight in shiny white armor out there for every princess. Otherwise you wouldn't be cornering me every chance you had to find information on our dead grandparents, who were some version of Romeo and Juliet—you claim."

The lump in my throat grew to a boulder, and I swallowed five or six times trying to dislodge it. "I… did have my happily-ever-after, and now it's solidly placed in the happily-never pile."

He raised an eyebrow. "I don't believe it. You're a keeper, Frances Burns. You're the type of woman men get a hold of and don't let go. Secure, independent but not flashy with it, supportive alongside it. Caring, unconditionally. Men eat that shit up."

"Are you drunk?"

A belly laugh rang between us. "No! I just know what I'm talking about."

"Well, I think my ex would disagree with you."

"Hmmm, an ex. Interesting, but not for now. Let's change the vibe. Where did your Paps grow up?"

"Finally, we can talk about what I want. Brooklyn."

He nodded. "Milly too," he added. "And tell me what you found. What treasures of their past?"

"Is that snark I detect in your tone?" I came right out and asked. "Are you mocking me?"

He reached over and took my hand in his and small fireworks played out when our skin touched. It was one of those moments you read about and thought was bullshit, but then it was happening to you.

"Never. I wouldn't dare not believe you and mock you." His fingers gave mine a squeeze meant to comfort me, but it was laced with sarcasm. He was definitely questioning if my mission was believable.

As I was about to open my mouth and tell him this was true for certain, the salad and an enormous plate of fried chicken and artichokes arrived.

Mack offered me the plate first, and I took a smaller breast before watching him grab a piece and take a bite.

"Mmm," he moaned, and under other circumstances it would have rattled my soul, causing me to be jealous because I wasn't the reason for the sound. There was a time in my life that I'd brought moans out of mouths. Or a mouth.

But we were getting to my part, my mission.

Taking a nibble of my salad, I chewed and spoke. "I found letters after my Paps died. One from each week of their dating, just shy of a year. They spoke of the days prior, noting their experiences together, almost like she was documenting their time and love for one another. Each one ended with what they had to look forward to, always including a family and making their own way. She started every letter with 'My Dearest James.'"

Mack dropped his chicken on the plate, wiped his slick hands on a napkin and stood. "You know what? I forgot I had to be somewhere. Don't worry about the bill, Corey will settle up with them. Enjoy your evening."

"What?" It was a whisper. My body was shocked—I was about to be deserted at a table for two. Definitely a first for me, and not something I'd expected out of Mackenzie Miller. I didn't know why; he was a bona fide jerk.

He certainly had not shown much of his softer side.

"Good night, Frances."

And in an instant, he was gone.

After a second piece of chicken, Luke approached and said the bill was taken care of, and asked if I wanted anything else. I didn't think they had peppermint bark ice cream, nor was I willing to display my addiction in public, so I declined his offer and took an Uber back to my apartment on the Upper East Side, falling asleep with my makeup and pencil skirt still on.

The next morning, after a strong cup of coffee, two trips to the bathroom, and a vitamin C mask, I made myself get to work. Where, luckily, I had a slammed day. Several of my regular customers had weddings to attend in July and August, and all wanted summer-weight suits and linen pants for the rehearsal dinners. My day was a constant stream of pulling the aforementioned garments, sizing and fitting the men who paid my bills, and reassuring them their clothes would be ready for whatever weekend celebration they had in the Hamptons. I was too busy to even think about how I had nowhere to be any weekend of the summer or how I was just about too old for the nuptials circuit. Then my cell rang.

I happened to be in the back, steaming a shirt, when it buzzed in my pocket, and I yanked it out.

The screen said *PRIVATE*, but that wasn't uncommon when it came to my clients.

"Hello, this is Frankie Burns," I answered, hoping there wasn't a wardrobe emergency on Fire Island. Some salespeople had been known to make house calls. Not me.

"Frankie, it's Corey."

With the phone tucked against my neck, this was a surprise, considering I didn't want to hear from Mackenzie Miller after being ditched, let alone his assistant. "Listen, whatever it is, I don't care. I'm at work, and it's clear your boss is a coldhearted jerk."

"He feels very badly about what happened last night."

I set the steamer wand down, fearing I might scald the fabric or my hand. "I don't care about what went down or Mack at all. Don't get me twisted—I'm all about this mission of mine. But not at the expense of my fragile ego."

"I don't know what, but something triggered Millsy. And even if I did, I wouldn't be at liberty to say. It happens from time to time, but he always rights it. Anyway, he asked me to call you and see if you wouldn't mind having the letters couriered over to him. He said you'd know what he meant."

I began to pace. "You're kidding, right? And you think using a cutesy nickname for the heartless man you call boss is going to help your case?"

"I can send someone to you, to pick them up—"

"No, you can't. I'm not parting with those. Your boss will probably light them on fire for funsies."

"Millsy doesn't do funsy."

"No kidding."

"Look, Frankie, I like you. I've said it before. Mack is complicated. I don't know what the letters are or what they mean, but he said to tell you he'd look at them himself so you can talk after. That's his offer."

I blew out a long breath, a strand of hair flying in front of my face.

"I don't accept the terms. And, as I said before, I'm over Mack. But if he wants to read the letters, I can bring them and sit in an adjacent office. That way, if I smell smoke, I'll know there's been foul play. That's my offer."

"I'll take it back to him. God, I adore you for him. It's like I picked you myself, but you fell out of the sky like manna from heaven."

I was about to argue—I wasn't manna, and I didn't believe in heaven… But I didn't have a chance because Corey hung up as soon as he was finished speaking.

CHAPTER Eight

MACK

I sat in my study, the tidy plastic box on the table in front of me. I was the opposite of tidy, sweating like I was working out despite the air-conditioning being on sixty-seven. I'd known there was no other choice but to agree to this arrangement.

Everything I accused Frances of being, I knew to be true. She believed in happy endings and fairy tales, and probably castles too. Although she wasn't the type of woman you could hurt and be easily forgiven. For every ounce of sweet running through her veins, there was venom in equal measure. If you cut her, she bit back. With fangs.

Corey handled the arrangements, sending a car to pick Frances up at her place and transport her to my apartment, letters in tow, the way she suggested. Actually, she'd offered to bring them to the office, but there was no way I could do this sort of thing in a public place.

Which was how I found myself sitting here in a fever pitch, on a Sunday no less, a week and a half after I'd deserted Frances. Of course she'd played hardball and said this was her first available date and she wouldn't be separated from her treasured letters.

Now she sat waiting in my living area, hopefully sipping the latte my housekeeper prepped for her before leaving. Magda usually took off Sunday for church and family, but I'd asked for a favor—one hour to help Frances get settled. Magda had looked at me like I'd spoken a foreign language. The ask was so unusual, she'd agreed.

In the current moment, I regretted everything about the day so far.

Unclipping the side of the container, I peered inside. Forty-seven letters, each one seemingly placed back in its envelope. Thinking she kept them in chronological order, I lifted the top one, sliding my finger inside the envelope and delicately pulling out the sheet of paper.

Noting the date on top, January 1ˢᵗ, I assumed this was the very first one.

My Dearest James,

Reading the salutation had me as unraveled as the first time I'd heard it spoken. I had been Milly's "Dearest Mackenzie" all my life, and to now hear she used that same sentiment for someone else shook me.

It wasn't jealousy, but rather shock. If I was being honest, I hadn't really put a lot of stock in Frankie's story before the exact moment she spoke about the letters. Sadly, she was hot and had piqued my interest, mentally and physically, so I went along with her ruse until she dropped the bomb on me—the *Dearest* modifier changed things. It proved she might be onto something, and Milly had held something close to her heart without telling me.

It also changed Milly's final letter to me and her wish for me to find true, everlasting love.

I shook my head. I couldn't think about my letter now when I had a stack of new-to-me ones I needed to get through.

Leaning forward, I cast my eyes on the letter again.

My Dearest James,

My resolution in the new year is to write a letter to you every week, so you don't forget me. Or us. The day will come where we can't be together. You know that, right?

After my first kiss, I will never, ever, ever forget you.

I can't believe you kissed me last night at midnight, hanging from my windowsill, but it's burned in my memory like the day we met.

I can't believe how many times I ran into the corner store for something my mama needed and might have seen you but didn't. Why? Because I'd been raised to be prim and not look at men. When I ran into your chest, it was destiny. Of course, I wasn't looking where I was going, and I knew the moment I hit your body that it was meant to be.

Meeting you has been the highlight of all my days.

I'm sorry I can't invite you into my home, and all I can offer is a perch on my window since my bedroom is in the back and private. It's the best I can do.

I love all our moments we steal away from watchful eyes, and I promise to bring Connie's and my special soup next time I see you. It's not fair that I'm allowed to be friends with Constance and not fall for you. It's a cruel world, but my papa would never allow it and my zayde would sit shiva for me. That means mourn my death.

But it's a new year, and maybe something will change in the way the world sees you and me. I just see us as two people who care about one another.

I am counting the minutes until we walk through the zoo like we talked about.

Until then, don't forget me.

Your Dearest Rosie

One letter, and my stomach was lodged in my throat.

Acid burned in my chest and a swell of emotions threatened to spill out from me. I hoped Frances stayed firmly planted on the other side of the apartment.

After being emotionally in check for decades, the cement walls I'd poured around me were about to be bulldozed by my grandmother's long-lost love story.

Closing my eyes, I swallowed and put the letter on the table and opened the next.

This one was more of the same. Why couldn't they love one another freely? Milly was already afraid of her parents learning of their affections…all of it heart-wrenching, and it was only the second letter.

They'd seen a monkey at the Prospect Park Zoo and secretly held hands while walking around. James had brought a pepperoni roll, not knowing my grandmother couldn't eat it, and she would never forget their combined laughter over it.

My mind spun with the details. Milly took me to that zoo when I was young; she didn't speak a word of going there in the past. It had been around since 1935, I learned from a quick Google search on my phone.

"Because she was Jewish…she couldn't…love," I was muttering to myself when I heard footsteps padding into the room.

"Mack, are you okay?"

Her words were soft, compassionate…while my eyes burned and my chest ached. "Please," I said, my voice gritty and angry and raw.

"Please what?"

I didn't know. My mind said to say *go*. My body said, "Stay."

My grandmother hadn't asked me to find love only because she wanted that for me, but also because she couldn't have it herself. And my dad had so royally messed up in that department, and I was beginning to think my grandmother blamed herself.

The sofa depressed next to me, and my brain wanted to violently scream at Frances to get out. Except my forehead met her shoulder, and I breathed her in, allowing all that she was to calm me.

Her hand ran along my forearm, goose bumps breaking out along my bare skin, and I was shocked at my decision to let it be. We stayed like that for a while—no syllables spoken, feelings swirling, and the air-conditioning blasting.

"Want to get out of here?" My mouth formed the words as my eyes connected with Frances's green orbs.

"Are you finished?" She took in the open letter on the table.

Shaking my head, I spoke. "No. I can't. Right now. Can I keep them? I see how special they are. I promise, I will not do a thing and I'll return them just as they are."

She nodded, her palm still singeing my skin.

"I'm sorry," I said, noting she wasn't answering my question about leaving. "I shouldn't have left you the other night. It was rude and inconsiderate."

Her gaze cast away from me, I caught a small tear in the corner of her eye.

"I won't do that again. I get why this is so important to you. It feels like a piece of history we're just discovering. Of course it only matters to us, but it is giving off paramount vibes."

She still didn't look at me.

My thumb reached up and swiped the tear. "I mean it. When I say something, I take it to heart. I'm sorry."

Finally, she met my eyes. "It was embarrassing."

"I know. I didn't think. It was immature." I'd hoped to not explain, but she wasn't leaving me much wiggle room. I couldn't help the laugh bubbling up my chest.

"What? You think this is funny?"

With her eyes narrow slants glaring at me, I shook my head. "No. Absolutely not." Taking her hand in mine, I asked, "Is this okay?"

I took her nonanswer as permission, knowing it was risky. We still sat next to one another, our thighs grazing since Frances had found me in a heap of emotions.

"I was hurt when you said how Milly addressed the letters—'my dearest.' You see, I was always 'My Dearest Mackenzie.' Never Mack or Macky or anything but Milly's dearest. When she died, the lawyers gave me a sealed letter written to 'My Dearest Mackenzie.' She left me with a bunch of instructions on how to live my life, none of which I follow too closely."

"And that's when you finally believed me? When I told you how she addressed my Paps?"

I nodded.

"I'm sorry if I hurt you in the process. And if it means anything, I'm sure Milly would be very proud of your success in life."

I couldn't help myself—my hand reached up and gathered her hair in its grasp and I gently pulled her close. My lips met hers. I didn't ask for permission, but her head tilted in, and her mouth opened for my tongue to enter…and I figured it was enough approval.

We stayed like that for a while, allowing some of the tension and need that had been hovering between us to seep out. Kissing, our hands traveling arms and cheeks, gathering one another closer. We couldn't get enough. I could smell one of our scents on her, not Milly's, and it tangled with my own bergamot mix. And the combination revved my engine. My hand slid up the back of her shirt and I felt my heart go from zero to seventy-five. Her skin was soft, delicate, and meant to be savored. My palm slid over her shoulder blade as my mouth continued to make sweet love to hers. I wanted more, maybe all of her, until I couldn't do it—

I pulled back.

"I'm sorry," I said for the millionth time this Sunday morning.

"Why?" She looked hurt—again by me.

"For doing that, taking us there, here, wherever we are. I'm supposed to be helping you, not hooking up with you. You're a gorgeous woman,

Frances. One of the best I've come along in this great big city. Milly might be proud of my business acumen, but not my personal life. I don't do long-term or commitment or forever. I learned a long time ago, from my mom, that love is fleeting. It's a me thing, not you."

This time it was Frances who stood and walked out, but not before grabbing the letter I'd been reading and stuffing it in her neat container and taking them all with her.

Without a word.

CHAPTER
Nine

FRANKIE

Coffee? Rachel texted later that week.

It was Wednesday and she knew I often left work a little early for kickboxing, and the Fourth was tomorrow. She knew I'd be free. *K. Our place, 4:30?*

That was all I could muster to write back. I hadn't been transparent with Rachel how off-the-rails this entire Mackenzie Miller situation had gone. The push-pull, the flirting and hurting in equal measure. The kiss, and his painful admission. I didn't know why it wounded me so much. It wasn't like I was looking for happily-ever-after for me…or my dream man. He didn't exist.

Rachel hadn't asked, likely thinking I'd listened to her and let the futile project go. So I shouldn't have been surprised when I walked into our favorite coffee shop and found her sitting at a table of people, including two women and one man. I'd bet anything the man was single and this was a setup. Rachel waved and I glared before ordering a soy latte. With my beverage in hand, I made my way to the table.

"Hi." Rachel stood while speaking. She was too chipper and anxious for my mood.

"Amber, you remember Frankie?" I nodded at Rachel's friend from the ad agency where she worked. "And this is Amber's partner, Robin. And their good friend, Oli."

It took all of my being not to roll my eyes. Oli, a funky hipster, was the last person I needed.

I knew my friend meant well, but I wasn't in the mood. "Nice to meet you," I said to the newcomers before turning to my phone.

"We are starting the holiday off early with a barbeque later on Oli's deck. Want to come?" Rachel flicked her hair and winked at me.

Oli was cute, with sandy blond hair, long around his ears. He probably was a graphic designer and a musician on the side. I noted a small tattoo on his pointer finger, a quarter note, and knew my suspicions must be correct.

"Oh, shoot," I faux exclaimed, staring at my phone, pretending to get a text. "A client left something at the store. I need to go retrieve it before they head off for the holiday."

Rachel eyed me suspiciously and asked, "Talk later? Or maybe see you at the barbeque?"

"Sure. I gotta go. I mean, I'll text you in a little. I don't think I can do the cookout. Bye, Amber. And Robin and Oli." My voice cracked in the middle, and I gave a halfhearted wave to make up for it and hurried out, no intention of following up with Rachel until the morning. As I knew, she could be pushy with her agenda but I loved her. Mostly.

Not wanting to waste my beverage, I took a walk on the High Line and settled in a rhythm of mindlessly sipping and overthinking until it was time for kickboxing. As I rushed into the studio, signed in and changed, I felt bad for the rest of the class with all the anger running through me; I was ready to kick through a wall.

And that was before I walked into the room and saw Mack standing there in his dumb black athletic shorts and gray T-shirt, chatting up

Roy. Well, he did look so handsome, and that angered me even more.

It wasn't like me to make a scene, but I couldn't help the loud growl and punch that emanated from me. The problem was my fist landed right in Mack's gut and he was now doubled over, threatening to puke by the sound of it, and I had definitely caused a to-do.

"Fuck, did you have to wound me?" Mack spoke through gritted teeth as I paced in front of him, waiting to see if he was okay.

"Apparently," I answered. "You deserved it, and now you're invading my space, my place where I find serenity. Why?"

We moved to the side of the room, without touching, a fissure of electricity running between us.

"I'm sorry."

"I'm sick of hearing that from you, and I was the one who walked out, I'll remind you."

"It was because of me." He finally stood and leaned against the wall.

I noted Roy started class without us. "You kissed me." I said that part softly, making sure no one heard me.

"No offense, Miss Priss, but this is New York. People kiss and have a good time, if you know what I mean, without it leading to marriage or blows. But not you. I couldn't keep it up without making sure you knew how I felt. And I was right. You ducked for cover before running."

"'Miss Priss'? You're seriously going to call me names? All because I'm not one of those people who gives my kisses out for free." I murmured the statement, but it was the truth.

He nodded. "I've never had a relationship last longer than a few weeks. It's not my style."

"How sad. You're what? Forty-five?"

He nodded again, making me worried he couldn't speak. "Forty-six."

"You deserve more than you think, Mack. I'm not saying with me, but your grandmother wanted that for you. I'm sorry about your mom. You got the shitty end of the deal."

"Did you just curse?"

Shaking my head, I said, "I'm going to join class before I kick you."

For reasons unknown to me, Mack followed me and participated too, holding the bag for my kicks. "I'd rather do this than be on the receiving end of one of those," he joked.

As sweat lined the nape of my neck, I didn't feel any better. There was no resolution. I didn't know any more about Rosie. But in the process, I felt myself falling for this man. A man who didn't believe in love or commitment or romance or really anything… He'd made it clear.

This very man interrupted my thoughts. "Want to do dinner?"

"Why?" I couldn't help the terse tone rolling off my tongue. "You confuse me." I was honest.

"You confuse me right back, if I'm being brutally honest," he said back.

"No dinner. Not tonight."

"Maybe another night?" he half stated, partially asked. He knew I was wavering, and that sucked.

I had to work on not being so readable, so I didn't answer Mack on his sort-of question. Walking toward the shower, I was still mad at myself. Of course I'd agree to another night because I was a goner when it came to feelings.

Which was how I ended up accepting a dinner invite less than forty-eight hours later.

I'd been coming out of the organic fruit market when my phone rang. It was a private number, and being a fool, I said, "Hello?"

"Hey," he said back, his voice gruff and hoarse.

My feet came to a dead stop on the sidewalk. "Mack?"

"Yeah, it's me."

I slid over toward the store's window so I didn't get trampled by busy New Yorkers.

"What are you up to?"

"Buying some fruit." I sounded like an idiot.

"Oh, yeah? Making a smoothie?"

I finally got my mojo back. "What do you need, Mack?"

"I was calling to see if you were free for dinner. Maybe a walk and dinner? A show? Whatever you feel up to…"

I tilted my head back, allowing the sun to shine on me, maybe warm my chilled heart. I'd spent the Fourth of July sulking and decided to not allow my mood to ruin the weekend. "Whatever? What are you talking about? You made your point. You don't do sentiment or long-term emotions. All I wanted was your help with my Paps. You can't even do that."

"I'm trying to make it up to you."

"Make what up?"

"I don't know. Can we just do dinner?"

"Why didn't Corey call?" I started to walk toward home. I had to allow some of the anger, want, need, and confusion to move out of my body.

"Because this is personal."

"But you blocked your number," I blurted out.

He laughed on the line, the rumble touching my nerves and flickering down my spine. "My number is always blocked. If it means you'll say yes, I'll give you my digits. You already know my address."

"Oh, that's an easy one to find. It's online. I even know how much you paid for your penthouse in Hudson Yards."

"Figures."

I countered his sarcasm with a question. "Do you cook?"

"Me?"

"Yes…" I was taking long strides, making my way home, fast and furious. Even though my brain said to slow my roll, my heart pumped a steady beat, wanting me to have dinner with Mackenzie Miller. And I needed to shower, change, and pluck my eyebrows before doing so. "You," I finished my thought. "You said your grandma was all about cooking. Do you cook?"

"No. Sadly, no, I do not cook. She would be disappointed in me."

"Okay, so let's cook. You want to have dinner? We can make it." Honestly, I had no idea what I was suggesting, but the fear of being dumped at a restaurant again—by Mack—loomed large.

"Ooookay, we'll cook. And the groceries?"

"Why don't you come up to my end of the island, and we can shop and then prep at my place."

"Are you inviting me over, Frances?"

"I guess I am…against my better judgment." Luckily, my small touch of sarcasm returned. "I'd hurry up and ask for my address before I change my mind."

"That's okay, I found it. Right here, on the internet."

"Touché. See you later?"

"Sure," he said and hung up before we could nail down a time.

I assumed he'd be over around five or six, giving me time to ready myself and my place. Heading back to the Upper East Side condo, my anxiety was hitting all-time highs. What if he didn't like my apartment? Or me? Oh wait—he didn't like me. He was doing me a favor, I reminded myself.

I was fluffing the pillows on the couch, still wearing my street clothes—jean shorts and white blouse with the sleeves rolled up and the bottom tied in a knot on the side—when the doorman called up.

What the heck? Looking at the clock, I noted it was a few minutes before four.

Opening my door, I said, "You're here."

"I was out when I called so I figured why not come over."

"We said dinner…are we having the early bird?"

He crossed the threshold, taking in my apartment.

I took him in—jeans, white T-shirt, sneakers, wide smile—he was unrecognizable from his typical staunch suit and firm smile.

"Nice place. I didn't take you for a UES lady with all the boxing and running off at the mouth. Little stiff up here for you?"

Ignoring me, he roamed the open living space, stopping to look out the window next to my treadmill, his elbow leaning on the side rail. "You use this?" he asked, an eyebrow raised.

"Yeah, I like it, when it's dark or cold."

"You take the classes or just run?"

"Classes. If you don't get credit or a blue dot, does it even count?"

"Didn't take you for a Pelo-junkie, but noted."

I noted he knew what a Peloton-obsessed person was.

"I like it here." He seemed to switch gears. "Feels like a good space. Homier than mine."

"Older," I corrected.

"That too. But less severe. Rounded edges and crown molding."

"Would you like some water? A beer? I think I have a few." I didn't want to examine my apartment; it was where I lived, but it didn't hold warm memories.

I turned toward the kitchen area, and when I was sure he wasn't looking I licked my lips, checking to see if I still had lipstick on.

I did.

"I'm up for a drink. You have a bottle of wine?" he said behind me.

Standing in front of the fridge, I thought this could not be weirder. The man had told me less than a week ago he didn't do commitments, relationships, or anything of the sort. Now he was here, unannounced, seemingly wanting to hang out. If I thought about it too much, I'd get a migraine.

"This your Paps?"

Turning, I saw him holding the picture I loved, but hated to share. "Yeah, right before he got sick."

"You look so happy here." His finger traced my face.

I nodded. "He wasn't," I blurted.

"Hmmm, a story there. Maybe open the wine first. Then, you can dive in…to both. The wine and the juicy tale."

"Did you want to go get groceries instead?" Sweat pooled under my arms. I opened the freezer pretending to look for something, cooling off. Checking my supply of ice cream and thinking it would be needed later.

"Why don't you tell me what we need, and I can send for it...then we can relax with the wine."

"No, you can do something like regular people," I pushed. "Not all of us send out for whatever we please."

Opening a bottle of white wine, I poured a healthy amount into a glass and looked at Mack. He nodded, and I gave it to him. It was part familiarity I didn't understand, and half weird as hell.

"Cheers," he said, making himself comfortable on the sofa.

"It's kind of weird you being here. Stalking me, I might add."

He chuckled and crossed his ankle over his thigh.

I found myself sitting on one of the kitchen stools across from him.

"The picture. Time to tell me."

"I was married." I said it fast, ripping the Band-Aid off. My close friends knew about my past, and well, I didn't welcome new people into my world very often. I guessed I'd brought Mack into my life unknowingly. "It didn't work out, end of story. No happy ending, like my Paps. Maybe it's the family curse. That was from my engagement dinner. I was so happy because I believed I was getting my fairy tale despite everyone saying it wasn't possible. My Paps for sure knew otherwise. He pretended to be excited for me, but I knew he wasn't. It was a bittersweet night. I was making one man happy and the other was miserable inside."

Mack nodded but didn't interject an opinion or pity.

"I got this apartment in the settlement," I somehow felt compelled to add. "So, you're right, it's not entirely me, personality wise. And also correct in that I couldn't afford it on my salary—originally."

"I didn't say that—"

"You thought it," I interrupted. "It was a parting gift following the worst few months of my life."

Again, he didn't condemn. "What happened?" He spoke like he actually cared, his tone soft, deep, but compassionate as he asked me about the darkest time in my life.

"Why do you want to know?"

He took a slug of his wine. "I told you my mom named me after a soap opera star. I mean, what nice Jewish boy is named Mackenzie? None. Maybe it was on purpose, I don't know. What I do know is I've not shared that tidbit with anyone. Why I picked you, I don't know. There are a lot of things when it comes to you, Frances, that I don't get."

After gulping some wine, I spoke softly. The words came out of me as if he was a trusted friend. "He didn't want kids. We didn't discuss much more than that. We were young, having fun, and he was making a lot of money. We both grew up on Long Island, and we were living the good life in the city. If I'm being honest, I thought one day he'd change his mind. Everything took a very dramatic turn when I ended up accidentally pregnant. The minute he found out, he left. Walked right out that door and filed for divorce."

I swallowed and looked up to find Mack on the stool next to me, his palm burning my bare thigh.

"I did what I could. Cried, tried to reason with him. But there was none of that. He was immovable on this issue. What's crazy is we grew up with one another, and I don't know how I never believed him when he said it."

Mack spoke. "I'm sorry."

"It's okay. We signed an early settlement agreement based on him taking care of the baby up front with a lump sum, but not being personally involved. The apartment would go to me. He'd made a huge hit on a startup, and he'd bought it outright."

"I'm glad you were taken care of."

His gaze roamed the room, looking for evidence of a child. With his brow furrowed, I could see the confusion in his mind.

"I lost the baby. Twenty-five weeks. After my sister helped me deliver a stillborn, my Paps made sure I still got everything out of the settlement, including part of the lump sum, even though I didn't have a child with him anymore."

I felt the tears fall before I could stop them from flowing.

"Frances." My name was a whisper on his tongue.

"It's okay. I'm okay now. I was working so hard, trying to prove myself in my job, and so stressed over being a single mom. I don't think I provided a very good home base for her. She rejected this life, and I'm at peace with it."

He gathered me tight and held me. The soulless man who didn't do commitments—that was who I poured my heart out to. Shows you, I never learned my lesson. Always trying to change people.

"No one deserves a happy ending more than you."

"This is my ending. All I need to do is figure out what happened with Rosie and my Paps, and that's it."

He shook his head and took a sip of my wine before tilting the glass to me. "Then let's drink to doing that."

I wasn't sure what to make of his sudden change in demeanor. I'd dropped a bomb in the middle of a war zone, and he was changing course. Maybe he was being sweet and diverting my attention. Or perhaps it was too much for him to deal with…

I assumed the latter when he suggested we go get the provisions and toast to our grandparents' story. All of a sudden, Mack Miller was compliant and congratulatory—it was confounding, yet I liked it.

CHAPTER Ten

MACK

"Add two tablespoons of the Dijon and two of olive oil. Two of each, okay?"

I nodded. "Bossy, much?"

She side-eyed me. "Next, whisk them together before adding a dash of pepper and some red pepper flakes. Got this? Whisk again."

Frances gave me step-by-step instructions, with me in her profile as she seasoned the filets with a dry rub. "Got it, coach," I said with a fist in the air.

We'd settled on steaks and some mustardy potato recipe, which was what I was currently working on, and a salad with warm, fresh pita. The last item because Frances was practically orgasming over the bakery counter.

"It's summer, and I didn't barbeque yesterday," Frances had stated in the small grocery store near her apartment. "We should grill," she'd mumbled to herself.

We gotten grass-fed beef and the ingredients for a side, and then we went to grab a baguette. That was when a moan of epic proportions had escaped her mouth.

"Warm pita, mmmm. My favorite. Do you care if we skip the baguette?"

"Frances, even if you weren't looking at me with your big green eyes full of desire and want—just to clarify, for the bread, not me—I'd say yes after hearing you moan like that. I'd say yes to anything…even you pulling my toenails off."

She'd laughed and promptly turned and asked for four pitas, explaining she'd freeze any leftovers. "It's the water," she'd said.

"I'm quite aware. New York water makes the best bagels, pizza, and apparently pita."

Frances dragged me back to the current moment. "Okay, toss that over the potatoes and pop the baking sheet in the oven."

I needed to remember this was a friendly night, not a lifetime commitment. Although it felt as seamless as one could be. The shopping, joking, cooking side by side…I'd never done that with anyone so easily.

"I'm going to go grill," Frances declared.

"I'm actually qualified to do that… We had a grill in college. The team used to grill out every weekend." It was an easier time, less pressure and even more limited reality. I'd been thinking about it a lot and how I should have embraced it more.

"I'd rather do it than be subjected to the neighbors' questioning later. They watch everything."

Off she went to grill the steaks on the common deck in the back of the building, and I was left to tend to the side dish and stare at the looming picture of her Paps. He was a good-looking man, despite his age in the photo. I could tell he had blond hair when he'd been younger and eyes the same shade as Frances. Deep green orbs that my grandmother supposedly loved at one point.

He wore a taupe suit complementing the pale pink sheath Frances chose for the event. Her eyes sparkled with excitement in the picture, a champagne glass in one hand and her Paps holding a tumbler of brown liquid.

I wondered who her husband was; there wasn't another name on the address when I'd googled her. My heart ached for Frances in a way I didn't know possible, and my head argued with me to turn the oven off and get out. But I couldn't. Problem was, I'd eventually hurt Frances too—because there was no positive ending in sight. We'd figure out the sordid details of our grandparents, all signs pointing to us falling for one another, and then I'd have to end it.

Yet I wanted to use my kickboxing moves and more on her ex-husband. What kind of asshole didn't want a child he took part in creating?

Oh right, someone like my own mother.

Which was why this whole scenario was even worse news for me. And why, despite the fun nature of college and being on the football team, I'd never been able to fully immerse myself in it. Because of her.

I sipped the chilled wine, allowing the alcohol to tickle my throat and dull some of my emotions. Except it didn't work—I wanted to ransack the place and look for evidence of the ex and go find and hurt him. It was irrational but it was happening.

Luckily, Frances showed back up with the steaks, and stated, "I'm going to let them sit for a few minutes while I whip up a salad. Can you check the potatoes? They're tiny suckers so they should be softening."

I was grateful for the small task but had to ask, "Um, how do I do that?"

There she went again with the type of laugh her whole body participated in, her neck falling back, exposing her smooth throat. I loved the blouse she wore; I wanted to rip it open and watch the buttons scatter all over the floor before running my tongue over her neck, down to her cleavage, nipping my way up, careful not to leave marks.

"You put a fork in one and see if it's tender." She said it before turning around and grabbing a container of spinach, her bun plopping to the side.

I did as she told me to do, and exclaimed, "Tender!" I didn't add that I was the opposite of soft, my hardened heart doing things it didn't ever do, and other parts of my body responding in very firm ways.

Another giggle from Frances as she tossed some spinach and cranberries and artichokes had my pulse flaring. She whisked—her word, not mine—a quickie dressing and tossed it all together.

Plating the steaks and salad, she instructed me to get the taters— also her word. And being the dog with a bone, I did what I was told.

"Wanna eat on the sun porch? We can take our plates and wine out. I have two stools out there," she said, somewhat hesitantly.

We carried all of our stuff out and I was looking forward to digging in.

Clearly, I had an affinity for good food thanks to Milly.

Then, not one bit shy or hesitant, she asked, "Tell me, what had you so deep in thought when I came back with the steaks?"

"There she is…my tiny sleuth."

"Come on, fess up," she said, sticking a potato in her mouth.

"The grilling had me thinking about the team, and that led to a dark time when I wished my mom would come to a game. I was the kicker—as you know—and I always hoped it would impress her. That's all. It didn't."

"I'm sure that hurt." Frances stopped eating and set her hand on mine. "I don't know how she didn't want to be at everything. I would have."

I nodded, saying, "I know," and ending this conversation. It was meant to be a fun night, and it was turning into one sad story after another. "Enough of my sob story," I stated. "Tell me what you did to ring in the Fourth?" I wondered if she'd worked, knowing it could be a big day for retail.

"Ring, not exactly. I had a quiet day, reading and relaxing. I make my own schedule and most of my clientele was either traveling or in the Hamptons this week."

I found myself admiring what a hard worker she was. Many people thought I'd been handed a golden egg with Silky. But they didn't know how difficult it had been to take over my family business. My dad not quite believing in me and the pressure to succeed were quite the cocktail to choke down.

"So what did you do yesterday, ride around on a private yacht, drinking champagne?"

I chuckled. Secretly, I loved the way she ribbed me. "No private yacht. Not my thing, especially on holidays. I'm pretty much a 'golf and head home' kind of guy on these types of days."

"What about the Hamptons?" she asked and took a small bite of steak. Another thing I found myself liking about Frances—she ate.

"I have a place, but I don't use it much. My aunt Susie spends a lot of time in the area, and I try to avoid her."

"Do you rent your place?"

I shook my head and had a gulp of wine.

"But you don't use it?"

"When I want, I do."

"Well, nice that you can just use it when you want and not have to rent it to make it all work from a numbers standpoint."

I noticed she was sensitive to money, likely from her settlement and bearing the weight of what it meant to have money from that angle. I didn't give a shit… I found myself tumbling fast for Frances.

I nodded, unable to come up with a good explanation from a *numbers standpoint*, other than I didn't need the money. All the while, I kept thinking the small square footage of a balcony Frances had been left in her settlement was the answer to my problem. A sliver of public space and a healthy dose of fresh air was good for me when it came to falling for the woman next to me. I also made a note never to have her over to my place (again) because this evening was going to end with my having this beautiful creature after dinner if I didn't get my shit together. And I didn't do dessert.

*T*he thing was, best-laid plans were never easy to execute, which was how I found myself the very next day, back in my study with Frances, with two coffees on the table, reading the remainder of the Milly letters.

At least I'd left my relationship with Frances firmly in the friend zone. The night before, I'd said good night after helping with the dishes, making up some excuse about an overseas zoom to Israel where they work on a Sunday. It happened occasionally for me, so not the end of the world, to tell a tiny white lie—right?

My Dearest James,

Thank you for the roses mixed with lilies. When I woke up and saw the bouquet of red and magenta in my window, all I could think about was you and when I could see you next. My heart pattered and beat a frenzy just thinking about you. Of course, I had to hide the beautiful arrangement in my closet, but I'm going to bring it out later to admire. And smell. I adore lilies, peaceful and energetic in their nature, and they smell best at night. Did you know that?

My mind went wild thinking about our company's original scent— Rose's Lily was its name. We'd always been in the skin care business, but my dad started the scent line around the time I was five. He'd been to a conference—I remember because it was the one time my mom stayed with me—and came back full of excitement over perfumes. He'd even brought my mom back some samples.

"What is it?" Frances sat across from me, reading a book, peering over the edge. She wanted to be there for support, but mostly she was here for any tidbits she could draw out of me.

"Silky's first scent was called Rose's Lily. I always thought it was a play on Milly's name, a tribute from my dad. But this makes it feel differently to me. Milly found herself involved in the business after my grandpa died. Well, she made sure she was, and this was her collaboration with my dad."

Frances nodded, a strange look across her face. "I wasn't sure if there was a connection, but I've seen older bottles of it. My Paps used to buy it for my grandma, which sounds atrocious but I guess it was his way of being close to Milly."

I nodded, not wanting to discuss how awkward that made it all sound. I read on, ignoring the woman possessing my mind. She still had a distant look on her face, but I chalked it up to the weirdness swirling the room.

My parents are being extra watchful after seeing us on the park bench.

I explained we are friends from the store, but they don't believe in girls and boys being friends, especially ones of different religions.

My Dearest James, I've explained to you that when I am ready to get married, I will go on meetings with a chaperone and my suitor. It seems outdated, but it is our way.

Although it's been like a dream to think about you being the suitor for a brief moment while we sat on the bench. Our five children running around our house, your customs and mine mixing and blending, our love and adoration carrying on forever.

For five minutes, we were in love in the open, for everyone to witness what true, true, true love is like. When two people love one another for their deep souls and beautiful personalities. That is me and you. Until we were spotted.

My dad said none of it is possible and that broke my heart.

I miss you, my Jimmy, and I will see you soon. Even if it's to say goodbye.

"I don't think I want to read the final letter. This was enough," I said, setting the next-to-last letter down on the coffee table.

"It's mostly more regrets and goodbyes."

"Too sad," I muttered.

She nodded but didn't move to my side of the room.

Her hair was down, smooth and glossy, but she wore her jean shorts and black tank top, a bunch of necklaces twisted around her neck. I liked the casual side of Frances.

"They definitely had a thing," I stated.

"Do you think your dad knew?"

"No. He and Milly were not fans of one another. They mostly fought. No way he wouldn't have dragged this in if he knew."

"I'm sorry." With those two words, she was on the move, coming close, her hand touching my arm.

"I'm not saying he didn't feel the effects of it. Maybe Milly resented him. I don't know. But he sought love from places he shouldn't. Like my mom. He became consumed with his love for her."

With the tips of Frances's fingers singeing my forearm, she spoke. "That's why you don't believe in love? Because your dad believed in it too much?"

Running my free hand through my hair, I took a deep breath. "She was the only person my dad loved. Samantha, that's my mom. Sami to my dad. Sure, my dad loved me, but not in a deep, soul-shattering way."

I watched Frances slide her hand down my thigh. It felt weirdly platonic and sensual at the same time; I needed space, and to be closer to Frances.

I was losing it, yet I kept going on with my emotional vomit.

"What I mean is my dad didn't care for me in the 'I would go to the ends of the earth for my kid' way. He did go to the end of the universe for my mom. Several times—looking for her when she disappeared once, then twice. First time, she was in Barcelona. After that, she wasn't as easy to find. She'd pop back up and go again."

"I can't imagine," Frances said, her voice raw and raspy with emotion.

"I knew you couldn't from just the way you spoke about your pregnancy."

A tear fell from her eye, and she waved her hand, signaling me to not bring up the subject.

My leg felt the absence of her palm and my heart broke at her not wanting to discuss what a wonderful mother she would have been.

"Milly was left to take care of me, and she adored me. She gave me the unconditional warmth kids crave, but I never saw her act that way with my dad. Maybe she never did. He looked for the feeling with my mom, and she couldn't give it to anyone but herself."

"You can't blame yourself for that. You could love and be loved."

Turning to face Frances, I stared at her for a beat or two. "No, I can't. But that's what is frightening about you. You make me think I can care for someone like that. You may be small, Feisty Frankie, but you are brave and hopeful and full of passion and optimism. It's a cocktail I want to get drunk on."

"I'm not...optimistic," she countered.

My fingers grazed her cheek. "So beautiful," I whispered. "I'm going to be honest. I don't fucking know what I'm doing right now. I can't—won't—spend my life chasing something that doesn't exist for me. Yet here you are, and you make me feel like it does. It's your optimism, raining over me. No one chases down their grandfather's love story if they're not a believer in all things positive. That's you, Frances."

Her hand came to my thigh again and I wished I wasn't in track pants. Shorts, boxers, anything where there could have been skin-to-skin contact would have proven better.

"I'm not—" she started to argue.

I interrupted. "I'm going to kiss you, and then we are going to brunch. Because if we don't...I'm going to say something brutally honest here...I'm going to fuck you. Hard and fast and furiously."

My hand guided her face toward mine and our mouths crashed as violently as I wanted to be inside her. Last time, our kiss might have been gentle. This wasn't. Twenty-four hours of want and need were bound in one long-ass meeting of the mouths. We didn't break for air to slow the pace. We went at it, gasping all the way. My tongue slid in her mouth, hers meeting mine. I couldn't get enough of her taste—minty and tainted with the hope I saw in her eyes. I wanted to swallow the feeling and all that was Frances.

For five, ten, fifteen minutes maximum, I wasn't jaded-and-cynical Mack, but a believer in peace, love, and destiny.

"I'm not going to break if you fuck me." That was what she broke free to say…

"Don't ever, ever say *fuck* again near me."

She raised an eyebrow.

"Because I'm trying to do the right thing, and hearing that kind of language from your Smurfette mouth does things to me."

She broke out into laughter. "Smurfette…that's funny," she said in between giggles.

"Come on," I said, standing, hoping my dick realized it wasn't getting involved with the blondie.

She took my hand, smoothing her tank with her free fingers.

"Brunch or bust." I had to get out of here.

CHAPTER
Eleven

FRANKIE

"The pink shirt looks handsome with the navy striped suit. Exquisite, if I may."

"Not as exquisite as it would if you joined me in a dress, on my arm, and attended the event with me. One of these days you're going to say yes, my darling."

He winked at me from the three-way mirror, and I pretended to coyly shy away from his attention.

"You know I can't, Baron," was what I said.

I don't want to, was what I whispered in my mind. *Especially now…*

Baron Andrews was a notorious flirt with extremely deep pockets. I mean, with a name like Baron, you had to be swimming in deep money and deeper family history, right?

He'd been one of my first customers, rushing in for a tie one rainy, slushy Tuesday. I'd only been working in the job for a few months, and I remembered the rain pelting and the slushy ground chilling me as I made my way into the store, thinking no one was going to shop today.

Right before lunch, Baron came storming in. He had a luncheon nearby and forgot a tie, and his assistant hadn't refilled his office with shirts and ties—whatever that meant. I had no clue back then.

I'd found him a dark green tie—it was holiday time—and noticed a snagged stitch on his shirt. We got him set in a new shirt, tie all centered and ready to command attention, "Little Drummer Boy" playing in the background, and off he went. The following week he was back to buy a few suits, asking me to play our song. *What song?* I hadn't a clue what he was going on about until "Little Drummer Boy" came back on, and he took me in his arms and swung me around.

Until then, Baron had been buying his clothes at another notable department store, he remarked, but he liked working with me. He'd been shopping and flirting exclusively with me for the last decade plus.

Which was why I couldn't afford for the other man striding into the department to mess up the arrangement. I still had to pay bills.

"Frances!" His voice rumbled through the air and tickled my nerves.

Baron's head perked up and he looked in the mirror at the spectacle behind him. Mack was approaching as fast as anyone could possibly do while weaving through a labyrinth of clothing racks and mannequins and displays.

"Frances!"

I swallowed whatever emotions were currently clogging my throat and said, "Mackenzie," firmly and matter-of-factly.

"Are you double-timing me?" Baron joked, turning to face me and now an impatient-to-speak Mack standing by my side.

"I need to discuss something with you," Mack said.

"Fashion emergency? I made an appointment. You should too," Baron said.

Funny, but out of line.

"Hey buddy, sorry. Just have to steal Frances here for one quick second. Looks great, by the way." Mack waved his hand in front of

Baron.

"Frances? Frankie, you okay? Need me to call someone?"

Now Baron was tightening our circle as Mack inched closer to my side.

"She's fine. I'm a friend. We know one another," Mack eyed Baron while he spoke.

"I'm in the middle of a sales appointment," Baron responded.

"I'm at work, Mack," I said, staring down the man of my recent fantasies.

"Are you Mack Miller?" Baron interjected, his energy and tone taking a dramatic turn.

"Didn't seem to bother you when I was at work…" This was directed at me. Mack had a point. I just didn't cause a cock-off when I interrupted him at the mall or his office.

Running a hand through his jet-black hair, Baron spoke. "Delighted to meet you. Baron Andrews," he said while holding his hand out. "Sorry for the gruffness. Can't have my time with New York's best men's clothing lady interrupted. You've been on my radar for a long time. My family is in the import/export business, and I always wondered who does your international shipping."

Mack reached into his pocket and pulled out a card. "I have a logistics person who handles it, but let's set up a meeting. Call my assistant."

I wasn't immune to deals being done in my department, but this was a whole new level of weirdness. Mack likely wanted to get rid of Baron, and would say whatever it took.

"Frankie, do you think the suede loafer? Or go total hipster in a sneaker with this?"

"Can I borrow her for one moment? Loafer, for sure," Mack interjected.

"Hmm, yeah, loafer. Okay, make it quick. I need to get a pair of jeans for another event. A soiree at the zoo… Maybe you'll say yes to that, Frankie. Go with me…"

Mack's mouth pinched, and I said, "Come on, make it quick." I dragged him toward the counter. "What's got your tighty-whities in a bunch?"

He countered my question with a question. "Are you dating that doofus?"

I side-eyed him.

"Answer me." His tone was authoritative and gruff.

"Why? You don't do commitment. I can date who I want."

Anger flashed in his eyes, followed by hurt, his mouth now turned down.

"No." I touched his hand with my fingers. "No, I'm not. He's a customer. And you're interrupting, you know?"

"Okay," he said before taking a deep breath. "My apologies. Look, this was urgent. Also, I don't wear white tighties, or whatever you said."

I couldn't help but laugh. "I didn't take you for a briefs kind of guy anyway."

"Boxer briefs. Good ones," he muttered.

"It's okay, Mack, you don't have to explain your underwear choices. Now what did you need?"

I had zero clue what was going on with us. It was Thursday. The last I'd seen or talked to him was when we had brunch on Sunday and he sent me home in his SUV, Alex driving and eyeing me from the front—checking that I was okay and not crying, I assumed. I wasn't sure if I should contact Mack or if he would reach out to me. He'd been pretty tight-lipped about the letters after we left his place, but I could tell he was affected.

"I found her…" He spoke softly, his eyes on me.

"Who did you find?" We hadn't even spoken about a *her*, other than his grandma.

I felt a headache coming on. Between the whiplash of everything that was Mackenzie Miller and his showing up at my work and Baron's posturing, I needed some ibuprofen or a margarita.

"Connie."

"Milly's friend? That Connie? Constance?" A firework went off in my belly.

"Yes."

"I haven't heard from you in days…I don't know why I blurted that out. I'm sorry. I'm not your keeper and you're not mine." Feeling myself spiral from the extreme emotions and happenings, I clamped my mouth shut.

"I had to go to London. I should've said something…and you're right, you don't need a keeper."

I should've been flattered or smitten or I don't know what with his ability to admit my independence, but I was too hung up on the first. "London? It's only been five days since I last saw you— Never mind. London, that's…I don't know what that is. Never mind, tell me about Connie."

He glanced over at Baron who was on the phone, no doubt with Corey, setting up a meeting with Mack.

"First, I told Corey about the letters. I hope that's okay. I don't have many people in my life I can trust, so I'm left with my overly personal assistant."

He looked to me for some kind of approval and I nodded. I should be rushing back to my customer, but this felt monumental. Not just Connie, but Mack's confiding in me.

"Well then, you know Corey, and he's literally a man on a mission, starring in his own reality television show. And when I left Monday night for London, he set about finding Connie. I don't know if he did any real work, and my schedule may be empty and correspondence unanswered, but he located the Constance Fiorello we read about."

"Where is she? Can we see her?" I felt flushed. Surely it wasn't normal to practically be coming out of my skin over this—bouncing on my toes, my heart racing—but it was all true.

"She's ninety-two but has her full faculties. I know because Corey called her. And when he mentioned Milly, she went on and on about how she loved her, and they were best friends until her awful father got involved. Her awful father being my great-grandfather."

I started clapping. "I'm sorry, I'm not cheering for your great-grandfather being mean."

He smiled. "I know. I'm just putting your package together with a neat bow."

"I need to go… Can you give me the information? I have to talk with her."

"What?" he asked as if he was offended, and another look of hurt flashed across his face.

"I mean, do you want to go?"

"Of course I do. That's why I rushed over here to give you the news."

Baron cleared his throat and I said, "Coming, promise."

"Saturday at noon." Mack spoke softly and directly at me. "Then we will go out to celebrate, so hold the whole day."

I didn't know what it meant, but I had no reason to argue. I had a date with Connie, and potentially with Mack too.

CHAPTER *Twelve*

FRANKIE

Saturday morning, I waited outside for Alex and Mack's giant SUV per a text I received the night before.

I'd expected Corey to send instructions, but instead it was Mack who communicated he'd be coming to get me on our way to a nursing home in Queens.

As I slid into the car, I ignored his masculine forearms peeking out from where he had his white dress shirt rolled up and the earthy cologne rolling off him. Noting he was in slacks, I took in my jeans and lightweight sweater. "Is this okay?"

"Of course," he said as if I was being ridiculous. "I need to atone for rotten men in my family generations before I was born. I need to look the part of a good guy."

"Oh come on, you don't really believe that?"

He took my hand in his and spoke. "I do. Now, let it be."

I didn't push. Instead, we rode in comfortable silence until Mack took a call.

"My aunt," he explained to me after. "My dad's sister."

"Oh! Maybe she knows something…"

"No." His tone was short and gruff. "Susie only knows what she needs to know. What fits with her agenda. Involving her would only make our mission a mess. She'd push to know why and how it might affect her, and ultimately how it can benefit her son-in-law, Tom."

I couldn't help the laugh escaping me. "I take it you're not close with Tom."

"No. Not in the slightest."

The car slowed and we were parked in front of a large building in Astoria. Alex came and opened my door while Mack exited the SUV on his own.

"Here we go," I said, and Mack wrapped his arm around me, bundling me in tight under his shoulder. I wasn't even sure he knew he was doing it. From the outside it looked like he was comforting me, but I knew differently. Mack was seeking security from his own rambling emotions.

We approached the information desk, now walking shoulder to shoulder-ish, signed into the facility, and the receptionist told us Miss Connie was waiting for us in the atrium. Armed with directions, we made our way there.

"Oh, my heavens, you look just like them!" Connie greeted us with an enormous grin from a wheelchair covered in glitter with balloons tied to the handles.

"Miss Connie," I said, "So nice to meet you. I'm Frances…" I bent down to embrace the woman I could already tell was a genuinely caring person.

"Jimmy Burns's granddaughter. I'd spot you in a crowd anywhere!" She put her palms on my cheeks and stared into my eyes. "Same green as your grandpa. Rose was wild for those eyes—a sea of grass, she'd say."

As I sat down in the love seat across from her, a birdcage in my peripheral vision, I wondered about Connie's family and if this was a good place. Typical me, I was already attached to a person I met moments ago.

"And Mackenzie Miller," she said, turning her gaze on Mack, who was sitting next to me. "Rose would occasionally write and include a photo of you. She was so proud of the young man you were becoming. Occasionally she would tell me about your college football games. She was so proud. She'd say 'a nice Jewish boy out there.'" Connie laughed. "That was so Milly, calling everything like it was."

Mack cleared his throat. "She wrote? To you? She never said a word to me. Or us." He seemed stuck on the notion his grandmother communicated with another person he'd never heard of.

"She did write. Sometimes more than others, but I always looked forward to it." Connie beamed another smile on us. "Look at you two! And you found one another. I can't believe it. It's like one of those holiday movies they play at Christmastime." Connie's gray eyes, shielded by thick glasses, passed between us. She smoothed her palm over her brown hair, likely professionally blown dry into a bob.

This was a woman with enormous pride, and I felt myself vibing with it.

"Frances here wouldn't take no for an answer," Mack said while cocking his head toward me. "The little rascal followed me all over the city, wanting to know about her Paps and Milly, until I gave in. I didn't have a clue what she was going on about until I saw the letters..."

"Oh God, I forgot—you all called Rose by that nickname, Milly. She was ahead of her time, ditching her God-given name. As a girl, she wanted to believe she could love anyone. As a young woman, she wanted to be involved in the business, and she tried. As a grown woman, she stuck it to your dad and that wife of his, raising you how she saw fit."

Leaning forward, Mack asked, "How is it you know so much about me and I'd never heard a lick of you until Frances came along with the letters my grandmother wrote to Jimmy? A million years ago, if I might add."

"Hopefully not a million. That would make me awfully old," Connie joked back.

Mack smiled, letting go some of the tension he'd so visibly been holding in his brow.

Connie clasped her hands in her lap. "Pardon the chair," she said first. "Broke my hip a while back, and my ankle before that, so they have me shoved in this contraption. Thank heavens for my great-grandkids who decorated it. Cuties come every Friday afternoon."

"It's stunning," I said, feeling Connie shine her warmth on me.

"My mind, it's all here, I want you to know. And I'm not telling any stories or lies." She pointed to her head, and Mack nodded.

Sensing he wanted an answer, Connie went on.

"Your grandma and I grew up in Brooklyn together. For some reason, Rose was one of the few kids in her neighborhood to attend public school, not yeshiva like the others. Other Jewish girls, I mean. Rose was always smart, and as a teen she helped with the books for your great-grandfather's apothecary. He owned a drugstore where they would mix elixirs and creams. That was before he got into the makeup business with your grandpa, Harold, as you know. Anyway, she and I went to grade school together and became fast friends. We stayed friends all through school. I'd go to Rose's and eat chicken soup and salami sandwiches, and she'd come to mine and sneak food that wasn't kosher. We developed recipes together. Always at my house."

"The soup!" I couldn't help myself.

"Yes, the soup. Jimmy loved our soup…"

A tear sprung out of my eye, and I blinked it back.

"We were the best of friends until everything went south with Jimmy. Max, your great-grandpa, blamed me. He said my friendship was bad for Rose, yelled at your mom over the public-school decision, and was convinced it was me influencing Ruth to meet a *shegetz*. I'd never use that word, ever. I knew it meant a non-Jew, and wasn't nice to use, but he did anyway, repeatedly, at the top of his lungs. Those words cut me. And worse, he forbid Rose to see me. Obviously, Jimmy was ousted, and one hundred percent not allowed anywhere near Rose. To insure he was out of your grandma's life, they sent her away."

Mack sucked in a breath. "I never knew any of this. How is this possible? This all happened after they were spotted on some park bench? I never knew, and Milly…she carried this around all her life?"

Connie nodded. "It was a terrible time. At first, Rose thought she could let sleeping dogs lie and her dad would forget she'd been seen with Jimmy. But only a few days after it happened, she was gone. Poor thing was only eighteen when they exiled her."

"Do you need a break?" I felt compelled to ask Mack without looking at him. From his profile, I could see his brow go back to being furrowed and his eyes scrunching.

"No. Please go on, Connie."

"They sent Rose to Philadelphia to live with an aunt and married her off to Harold before bringing both back and working poor Harold to the bone. Harold was a smart one and had connections to build the business. It was all arranged through a matchmaker."

I saw Mack shaking his head. "I'm sorry." He uttered the same sentiment he'd said to me several times. "You lost a good friend, and my family acted in a way…not a very nice way, let's say. I can't believe this happened. I'm not insinuating you're making it up, but Milly never spoke of it. My dad never mentioned it. I don't even know if he knew…"

"It was the way the world was then. Part of me empathized with your great-grandparents after I had my own children. They'd seen the Holocaust and were so worried their culture and customs would be annihilated. But here's the thing about Jimmy, he would have agreed to anything for Rose."

"I get that it was a different time, but it's so far from how Milly was. Despite all this happening to her, she believed in romance. My dad made a mess of his own life and Milly still hoped for me to love whoever I was meant to do that with..."

"You see, Rose had just turned seventeen when she met Jimmy. It was a chance meeting and the two of them made it a point to sneak off as much as they could. When they were spotted, Max was so swift in his ending it all and shipping Rose off. But Jimmy, he hoped she'd come back and they could run off. They always believed in everlasting love, but then she returned with Harold. Poor Jimmy watched the couple from afar, and then your dad was born. That's when Jimmy left. He met a nice girl from right where we are in Astoria. Your grandmother," Connie said, nodding at me.

"They moved to Long Island after they were married," I filled in.

"Of course. I know, sweetie. I kept in touch with Jimmy and Sally a little. Every so often they would come back to Brooklyn to see Jimmy's parents and I would run into them. Sally had been a secretary at one of the businesses Jimmy called on. Together, they opened a furniture supply store on Long Island. She kept the books, and Jimmy called on the accounts."

"It's still in the family. My dad ran it, and now a cousin on my mom's side is in charge. My sister and I didn't want to work there." I felt a tug in my heart. Maybe I should have taken on the family business and not gotten caught up with Jeremy and his grand promises.

Connie filled in the silence. "My husband, Tony, may he rest in peace, never knew Rose or Harold or about Jimmy. I kept it to myself. Tony was an accountant, a good man and dedicated father, but he wasn't one for gossip or stories. We had five kids, and my daughter, Iris, lives here in Queens. That's how I came to be here."

I noticed Connie's nails were painted and thought her family must take good care of her. Manicures, wheelchair decorations, and balloons—this woman was loved and adored.

"Your grandma would write me letters. That's how I knew a lot, Mackenzie. She started to write in secret after she and Harold were married, and continued until around the time she passed. She'd send mail, but we never saw one another in person. I think she lived with the fear of losing me again."

"I-I…" Mack stuttered, and I couldn't believe what I was witnessing. The staunchest of men had been rendered speechless. "These letters… she seemed to write everyone but me. Only one, when she died."

"She loved to write. She practiced her handwriting nonstop in middle school—"

"She insisted I learn cursive," Mack interrupted.

"She told me," Connie said with a smile. "In one of her letters. In the beginning, she didn't write too many details. Your dad was a fussy baby, and she was devastated to be pushed to the fringes of Silky as it expanded. But as your dad grew up and settled, and then Susie was born, she wrote more in-depth. It was her outlet. She never said as much, but I could tell. I was the link to a part of her life she'd never have. Keeping me on the fringes, yet still involved, was her sliver of love and freedom. 'My Dearest Constance, my lifelong friend' is how she would start every letter."

"Do you have them?" I couldn't help but blurt out.

Connie shook her head. "She said at the end of every letter to rip it up and toss it. She always worried Tony would see the letters and alert someone. She didn't even know Tony but feared anyone knowing where her heart really belonged. With Jimmy. To my knowledge, Harold never knew about Jimmy. It was part of the agreement with the matchmaker. Find a boy from somewhere else who doesn't know about the shame Rose brought to the family." Connie tsked. "She lived with such a burden."

"I'm so glad she had you for all those years. It sounds like it was really meaningful to Rose, and was an outlet she needed." I tried to comfort Connie as my heart ached for a woman I never met. "How could she love a man as long as she had and never get to hold his hand ever again?"

Connie looked at me with softened eyes. "Rose never was the same when they tore her away from Jimmy. Losing me was hard too, but she found a way to know me and my family through the letters. Her dad always had an eye on Rose after Jimmy. Calling, checking. And when he passed, Rose was so used to living her life in fear of someone knowing her sin. Sadly, she never really loved Harold, but she believed divulging the truth would bring a bad omen on her family."

"I'm not sure we didn't have one anyway…a bad omen." Mack tried to crack a laugh.

"Psssh." Connie waved her pudgy hand at him. "I know all about your dad and his mistakes. Rose said it was her fault because she didn't love Jake enough in the beginning. From what I gather, she had a hard time attaching, especially with his fussiness and heart being so messed up. But that wasn't it. She took care of Jake and later was very supportive and close to him. Harold was a firm one. *Work, work, and prayer* were his lifelines. He didn't help Jake in the 'learning how to form a relationship' department, and Samantha was Jewish, which was all he cared about. He'd promised Max. Rose poured this all out in a letter around the time your dad proposed to Samantha. When your mom left, Rose wasn't surprised."

"My grandmother told me to find my person and hold on to them. In a letter, of course."

"Well, that's what you should do, honey. Maybe here with this sweet little Frances." Connie's gaze ping-ponged between the two of us.

"Not us," I said first, and Connie raised an eyebrow over her glasses. Mack didn't interject.

I filled the pregnant pause. "My Paps talked about his Rosie, especially as he got older. He never forgot her."

"That was Jimmy, the most caring man you ever met. He loved your grandma too. That's how big his heart was. I guess not as much as Rose, but his feelings were genuine."

A nurse came in and interrupted. "Connie, I'm sorry but you have

PT."

I was grateful for the respite. My heart was aching in a way I didn't know possible.

"Listen, come back," Connie said, reaching forward and taking my hand.

"Can we?"

"Of course."

"Do you have the recipe for mishy-mashy soup?" My mind was working overtime. I'd found a connection to my Paps.

"I sure do! Come back and we'll make it. That man, the one who called me?" Connie looked at Mack.

"Corey," Mack offered.

"Have him call again, and I can give him the ingredients for you to bring."

"Will do. Thank you." Mack leaned over and gave Connie a hug, his cheek lingering next to hers. I sensed he was having an emotional moment, and I let him have it.

Some strange concoction of sadness, despair, and confusion swept over me. I'd found a connection to my Paps—wasn't that what I wished for? Yes, but did that mean my time with Mack was coming to an end?

Wasn't that also what I wanted?

I gave Connie an equally long hug as Mack's and whispered "Thank you" in her ear.

She squeezed my side.

"I can't believe it," I said to Mack after Connie was wheeled away. "They loved one another all their lives and never got to be together." Wistfulness blanketed my words.

"And my family never knew..."

"She was protecting you, in her mind. It seems like she felt nothing good ever came out of people knowing. She lost Jimmy. And Connie, for a while. And lost the ability to love."

Mack frowned as we made our way out of the building. "I come from a loveless place. Now everything makes sense. My inability to love…"

While I was thrilled to get some information, I started to see how this visit wasn't positive for Mack. He wasn't himself in the car either, not mentioning the celebratory dinner he'd spoken about the day before.

Pulling up in front of my building, he looked up. "No way Corey isn't inviting himself to make soup with us," he said laughing, clearly trying to break the moment.

"No way! He will be there," I agreed, wondering if I should get out or wait for Alex.

"Get you at four? I want to go see something before dinner."

"Oh," was all I could say.

"Great!"

Walking into my apartment, I had no idea what he'd planned or what I should wear, and I didn't care. That was Mack to me. My *I don't care as long as I am with him…*

And I was in trouble.

CHAPTER
Thirteen

MACK

"*I*'ll get it, Alex," I said as we pulled up in front of Frances's place for the third time in one day. I was sure she could get around the city on her own, but something about this damn woman brought out the protective side in me.

Jumping out of the SUV in my jeans and white polo, I walked around the back of the car to open the door for an approaching Frances. She looked absolutely delectable in white cutoff shorts and a red off-the-shoulder sweater, her tanned skin exposed. I thought back to her kickboxing and the way her muscles flexed…

"Sorry I ran late," I said, breaking my moment.

"It's no big deal, you texted…" She climbed into the car, her ass in my face, and I made a note to never let anyone else open the door for her.

The truth was I'd had to collect myself after meeting Connie. I wasn't sure if I could reconcile Max, my great-grandfather, even being my family. *Who the fuck sends their own kid away for falling in love?*

I set my feelings aside as I rounded the car and hopped in the back.

"I didn't know what we were doing, so I hope this works," Frances stated, waving her hand in front of her outfit.

"I wasn't entirely sure either, but I made some calls…another reason I was late."

Alex drove toward the helipad and Frances watched out the window, not knowing where we were headed.

"You okay, after today?" she turned toward me and asked, her expression soft.

"Yes. It was…a lot. I'm sorry for you, that you had to hear that about my family. I wish Milly had told me, let me know what went down. I look like a fool for not knowing. Somehow, it feels like I could have protected you before these ugly truths were exposed. I'm a little ashamed and sad for her…but I get it was the way they handled things in that time."

I rambled and Frances took my hand. We stayed like that, her thumb rubbing mine, until Alex stopped the vehicle and I'd calmed.

"Helicopter?" Frances spoke, looking out the window, noting the helipad.

I nodded. "I figured we could have dinner in the Hamptons, make sure there weren't dust bunnies attacking my place. You seemed worried for me."

"Should I have worn something dressier?"

I shook my head. "That's perfect. If it's okay with you, we're staying in and someone is coming to cook. If you want to go out, we can, but this gives us time to unwind and not rush."

She nodded. "Sounds dreamy."

I couldn't help but think it was dreamy just having her with me, a thought I'd never believed I'd have. Then again, I never thought I'd send Corey an SOS text to find a chef and have him or her hightail it to my Hamptons place.

Corey was oohing and aahing and having a small orgasm over the phone when he called me. Luckily, he'd arranged a few catered lunches out in Southampton for me, and it was an easy task for the jack-of-all-trades in my life.

Now, as I opened the door to the helicopter and Frances climbed in, my heart rate spiked. My mind lived somewhere in between this being a huge mistake and the best thing I ever did. Seated, buckled, headphones on and prepped on safety, we were lifted into the air by the pilot. It was a short ride, and I took in Frances keeping an eye below us. She was smiling so wide, it hit her eyes. I wasn't sure who the excitement was for, but for a moment I allowed myself to believe it was me.

I couldn't help but lean in and kiss her neck, making my way to her cheek, and finally, her lips. It was messy, and our headphones kept invading one another's space, but for a hot moment we said what couldn't be spoken with words.

Breaking free, we stared at one another, my thumbs caressing her face. We didn't speak, despite feelings swirling all around us.

Much later, situated over a cocktail on the back porch while Serena, a local chef, made dinner, I said, "You know, I thought this whole chase of yours was kind of nuts."

She laughed; it was throaty and did things to me I wanted to ignore but couldn't. A silent growl to protect and savor this woman roared in my chest.

"I know, I know. It was a little nutty on my part. Still is. But I have to stay on this goose chase for my own closure. Thankfully, my parents are enjoying retirement in Florida and don't ask what I'm up to. Although…I'm truly sorry for involving you. I didn't mean to expose parts of your life you didn't want to know about or that made you feel bad." She ran a hand through her hair and I wanted it to be my fingers.

So much of this woman was still a mystery, yet there was a piece of yarn connecting us in an undefinable way. "You don't say much about your family other than your Paps. Tell me about them, now that you know all the dirt on my great-grandfather…"

We sat on padded chairs catty-corner from one another, and the hand she wasn't holding a drink with squeezed my knee.

"Max isn't you…"

I swallowed the guilt that had been lodged in my throat. "It's part of my family's legacy."

"Like Connie said, my grandma was Sally, and my Paps, well you know all about him by now." Frances switched subjects back to my question, somehow knowing she wasn't going to be able to change my mind when it came to Max.

I nodded. "Good ol' Jimmy, lucky in life, loser in love," I said.

"Truth," Frances agreed. "Anyway, Jimmy and Sally only had one kid, my dad, James Jr. My grandma worked hard with my Paps to run the business. All the pictures of my dad as a baby are of him in a playpen in the back office or being carted around the store in my mom's arms. And the yearly Christmas photo in the sofa section with Santa. Most kids were taken to the mall, but Paps brought Santa to the store. My dad continued the tradition, and it became a big thing to come to James Furniture to get a pic with Santa. He'd advertise the big event and it was a real see-and-be-seen for our neighborhood. It was good for sales too."

"James Furniture, huh?"

She nodded.

"Promise not to get too excited and jump in the pool naked?" I felt an eyebrow raise as I asked her. Being with Frances was fun, easy, natural—whatever word you would use to describe a relationship that felt good.

A giggle escaped her. "Yes, I swear!"

I loved the ease with which we ebbed and flowed between the serious and silly. It felt comfortable, like a worn-in glove, one you could easily slip on. "Unlike you, I haven't investigated you fully. So I didn't know about James Furniture. But now that you say it, I have a recollection.

When I was around ten, Milly took us there. It was wintertime, and she had her driver take us to Long Island. I remember it being a long car ride and we played tic-tac-toe in the back seat on an old tablet. When we got to the parking lot, Milly had her driver take me for fast food while she went in to order an armoire. I had no idea why we drove that far for a piece of furniture, and I was mad because I saw the sign for Santa and wanted to go in. 'We don't celebrate Christmas,' Milly said. It was one of the few times, she ever spoke sternly to me."

"Wow. I wonder if she saw Paps…"

Serena interrupted and asked if we were ready to eat, and we moved to the outdoor dining table, overlooking the pool. I carried our drinks, which Serena's assistant quickly refreshed.

"Don't forget where we were. I want to hear more about your family." I was happy for the break in the scene. I didn't know why I went there with that memory…reminiscing about Milly maybe going to see Jimmy… It was opening Pandora's box. There was also the mention of the armoire now, sitting like an elephant in the room. It was only a matter of time before Frances inquired about the gigantic piece of furniture.

As we sat, Frances took the hint and asked, "What about you? Like you said, I know you don't do Santa, but what were your holiday traditions?"

This made me chuckle.

Frances took a bite of her fish and hummed her pleasure. I didn't make it, but the fact that I'd provided it did something to me. I wanted to please Frances in a way I never wanted to care for someone. "Not much. When I was young, we fried potato latkes and doughnuts. As you know, Milly was big into the kitchen and making everything herself. My dad always had his assistant buy me the latest and greatest toys or video games. When I got to be around eight, they started dragging me to the office holiday party. That was my consolation for not having a mom—I got to go to the adults' celebration. I'd sit in the corner in my navy suit, downing Roy Rogers. You know what they are?"

"Of course I do. The male version of a Shirley Temple! Sugary cherry juice and Seven-Up. I used to order mine with extra cherries. By the way, since you never got to do it, this year I have to take you to meet Santa. He can talk to Hanukkah Harry on your behalf." It was silliness, but it was pure Frances, taking a painful moment and making it better.

I told her it was a plan and that I was hoping for a Lego set before conversation moved into safer territory—whether ties were coming back in style.

"I feel a bit targeted… I don't like ties…"

"That's because you don't need one for people to take you seriously. Most men need one to keep others in line. You do that with a look."

The chat could have taken a turn toward dirty talk, but I kept it PG.

*A*fter dinner, we got a ride to the inlet and took a walk on the beach, our hands easily slipping together. I felt Frances lean her head on my shoulder and I stopped in my tracks. Turning to face her, I couldn't find the words. It felt right…and beyond wrong…because I'd never wanted this or felt I'd deserved it.

"Why do you always call me Frances?" she asked, looking into my eyes. It was a welcome distraction from what was going on in my head.

"If everyone else calls you Frankie, I want to be different. Because it's…something else between us. At least for me it is. You see, you're this outstanding contradiction of a woman, *Frances*." I let her name roll off my tongue, savoring each syllable. "You're funny, sarcastic, bossy, demanding…all the above." I looked for the right words. "Sensual and smart and sexy as fuck…"

"You mean just plain sexy, right?" She pinched my side while interrupting me.

"No, *sexy as fuck*." I piggybacked off her comment. I knew she was kidding, but I couldn't help myself. "Ever since you blasted into my life, I can't get you out of my head. I want you, but I don't want to hurt you. I can't keep you, even if I don't think I can let you go. It feels so complicated."

Despite my trepidation, my lips grazed hers.

"What about your date? It didn't go well?" she asked, breaking free from my mouth, going back to weeks ago.

Not going to lie—her tone, laced with the smallest hint of jealousy, made me feel ten feet tall. It was my turn to give her a tiny pinch on the side.

"What?" She looked at me, eyebrow cocked.

"My date was a favor to a friend. And it ended up with me coming home early and thinking about you."

As the sun began to set, I could still make out the blush on her cheeks. I ran a finger over one, and she pulled away playfully. "Don't tease."

"I'm not," I whispered. "I like you, Frances, in case you couldn't figure that out. I didn't want to, but you're irresistible."

Cradling her face, I kissed her instead of waiting for a reply, her lips supple against mine, her tongue ready to tangle and her body pliant in my arms.

I wanted the moment to go on forever.

I was starting to think we could stay overnight—Frances seemed to love the bungalow—but my phone rang.

"Damn Corey. Bet he needs an update," I murmured, pulling my phone out.

It wasn't Corey.

"Dan?"

"Hey, boss. I hate to disturb your weekend but we had a problem out in Westchester."

I stepped away from Frances, mouthing *I'm sorry* and holding up a finger, signaling one second.

It took a bit longer than a minute as Dan, my head of security, said our store was broken into along with a few others in a mall. Normally, it was something Dan's team would handle and send a report along in the morning. But since this one was so close to me, they'd called.

I decided to go see the scene, cutting my evening with Frances short.

Call it work or self-preservation, but both had to be done.

CHAPTER
Fourteen

FRANKIE

The summer heat licked at my exposed back as I pushed myself up the far side of Central Park. My feet struck the pavement quietly, and I dreamed of the iced coffee waiting for me at the end of this run.

I wasn't always a runner...

When I lost the baby and my body had healed but my mind was still stranded in disbelief, my therapist suggested I try it. At first it was a futile effort, the solo exercise leaving me alone with my destructive thoughts. But after a while, I thrived in the moment. Kickboxing came next. And between the two, I began to gain composure, quieting my mind and controlling my despair.

I'd crafted a life around my fitness and work. I'd never be a mom or a wife again, but I was good at my job and building a small circle of friends and spending time with family. Paps and I had dinner every Sunday after Jeremy walked out, and we continued to do so even after I lost the baby. My parents didn't understand how I could be so upset with the generous settlement I received, and went about their lives as if I wasn't suffering. They'd told me to suck it up and enjoy my windfall—I couldn't even believe they raised me, let alone created me.

My sister had been with me during the stillbirth, forcing Rachel out. Ashley only put up with me as long as she could take; she was young and wanted to live life. *I bogged her down*—her words.

Thankfully there was Rachel, who stood by my side, came over to watch movies, and rubbed my back when I needed it. When I first started to run, she'd join me occasionally, dragging me for coffee afterward, which turned into brunch or lunch or dinner. It was in this tiny cocoon that I healed.

I was mostly happy, except for the nagging need to understand the secrets Paps had shared with me. To me, the discovery was the special sauce for my own long-term happiness.

Recently, I'd leaned on Rachel again. We had dinner a few times in the weeks since Mack ran out on me…again. I wasn't sure if it was good or bad luck, but my parents had recently reached out, wanting me to visit. I'd declined. They had no idea what I was up to, and I didn't plan to tell them.

Today, dependable Rachel was back to Frankie duty, meeting me after my run like in my hellish days when my life fell apart.

I'd regretted pushing Mack into my never-ending chase. He'd only been hurt in the process, and I never wanted him to be collateral damage. The guilt gnawed at me as much as the knowledge of the mystery armoire, and all of the above started to play mind tricks on me.

"Let it go, Frankie," Rachel told me over my iced vanilla latte. "He's a grown man. He's fine."

We strolled outside the coffee shop, cups in hand. "I can't. I mean, there was so much happening. We had a real connection, and I felt like he was also vibing with my mission. But then, I don't know…he wasn't."

She peered over her giant hot coffee at me. "Don't you think he may have been humoring you a little with a mission? I'm sorry, I hate to be a Debbie Downer, but it seems like a waste of time for a rich bachelor like him…to be into all that."

I sniffed back some sweat, thinking carefully. "He said as much. At first he thought it was trivial, but then he got into it. He even remembered the furniture store. I don't know, something spooked him and it's my fault. I hate disappointing people or adding to their pain. You know this."

She took my hand and squeezed, "Frankie, babe, maybe it's a sign. Like it's time for you to date. Put your grandfather's love life behind you and worry about your own. You liked Mack, you will like someone else. A blessing, as my bubbe would say. Your heart will love again."

I felt my head shaking side to side while an ache settled further in my heart.

"It's okay to want love for yourself." Rachel side-eyed me, not willing to look me straight in the face.

"I'm not you. You put yourself out there," I admitted. Rachel was divorced too, but had no kids and was enjoying the dating life at thirty-six. "Maybe those two years make a difference. At thirty-eight, I'm plain old."

"They don't. Look, Mackenzie Miller is a catch, but he doesn't want to be caught. He's elusive. He read your letters, introduced you to this Connie character, and let you know his grandma continued to carry a torch for your Paps. Why else would she go to the store? It's enough, I think. They were in love but it was forbidden. There you have it."

The sun was high overhead, making me feel warm, yet a chill ran down my spine when she said forbidden. Like Mack, I didn't understand how something like that could be tolerated.

My errant thoughts were saved by the bell—my phone dinged. Every time a text came through, the same icy-hot feeling invaded my body. Of course I always thought it might be him. It had been two-plus weeks since we'd been in the Hamptons.

He'd texted once to apologize and another to say he was off to London again.

Now, I yanked my phone out of my running armband to see who was bothering me on a Saturday.

I'm going to Westchester tomorrow. I have to grab something at the house. Do you want to see the armoire?

That was all he wrote—as if we'd been chatting regularly over the last several weeks and he didn't ditch me in the Hamptons—yet my heart rate was through the roof. The thing was, I didn't know if it was because of Mack or the prospect of finding out more about Rosie and Paps. The two had become so intertwined, and I couldn't figure out if I was falling for Mack or felt certain ways because he held the keys to more information. The former spoke to me; I was into Mack for more reasons than one. Except he was a train wreck, running away when he got scared, afraid to face reality. And also hurting because of me. The entire scenario was a crash-and-burn if there had ever been one. Maybe because Mack wasn't meant to be caught, like Rachel said… Everyone knew I was stubborn though, and when I wanted to believe in something, nothing deterred me.

"Well, who is it?"

I looked up to see Rachel staring at me. Shoving my phone away, I couldn't lie, so I said, "Him. He wants to see the armoire tomorrow with me."

"Well, there you go. Another information-foraging date with the man. Hope you get what you want because if he deserts you again, I'm going to ban him."

I didn't doubt that. When Rachel put her foot down, she was not movable.

Part of me wished she would ban him now because whatever was blooming between us wasn't an annual. It was a perennial, in season, and would be dead by the first frost.

"Morning," he said, holding the car door open for me.

I nodded.

"I'm sorry," he said when he got in the car.

"Save it. You have said that to me so many times, it doesn't mean a thing. I'm sorry this, and I'm sorry that…" I turned to face him. "You know what?"

"No, but I'm sure you're going to tell me." His mouth quirked… damn him.

"I want to slap that smirk off your face. The last thing you are is a wet noodle. You're Mackenzie Miller, a powerful man who doesn't do commitments. So just stop with the 'I'm sorry' every minute. If it gets the slightest bit deep or heavy, you cut and run. Let's keep this simple—I want to know about my Paps and you're helping. No feelings needed or required."

He kept his gaze on me, taking my lashing, allowing me to finish.

My chest felt heavy with memories I didn't want to be having, and pain I'd suppressed long ago. "In case you forgot, I had a man leave at the worst time possible. Sever ties, and leave his baby for freaking good. He didn't know she wasn't going to make it. The thought of a family was just too damn deep for him. I'm not looking for any of that BS anymore—"

He snatched my hand in his and caressed my fingers. "Shh." He silenced me with his commanding tone. "You're right, I'm not a cut and run type, as you put it. Yet that's exactly what I've done. You know why? Because the only woman I ever truly cared about was Milly…until you. You pull me in without knowing it, and I push you away, unable to control how I'm feeling. I'm trying, but you have to understand I don't like the lack of control."

I sighed and he squeezed my hand. It might be New York's best-kept secret—this man was broken beyond repair.

"Mack," I managed to breathe out.

"I did have to go back to London," he cut in. "Their department stores can be very demanding, and we are trying to play nice since we are opening a perfumery there. We don't want them to see it as competition, so there have been many talks. And the Westchester store is our model for London, the layout and all that. And while it being broken into wasn't because of the design, it reflects poorly on the brand. Luckily, it was a multi-store incident at a mall, and the person of interest was apprehended."

I nodded, thinking how quickly he'd changed subjects. This man really did like controlling the dynamic.

"A girl? You were having a little girl. I'm so sorry that happened to you." His hand was back on mine, soft eyes focused on me, and his tone gentle and compassionate.

The way he'd whipped back to what I said made my head hurt from the change in emotional altitude. I'd missed a few therapy sessions, and I was thinking it was time to schedule an emergency appointment.

I looked toward the front, and Alex was fully concentrating on the road, taking us to Mack's childhood home.

"A girl," I confirmed. "I planned to name her James for Paps and Dad. It wasn't in style to use James for a girl when I was born. She was a beautiful baby, even though Ashley said she looked like an alien…"

"Oh, come on. An alien? Who would say that?"

"My sister. She's younger, and a bit of an oddball. Flighty, but she was with me during the birth, and she did her best to be supportive in a way she didn't really know how to be."

"Does she live in New York?"

I shook my head, saying a nonverbal prayer that we'd moved on from my baby who never lived a day…

"She's in Scotland, my sister," I explained. "Fell in love with a bartender when she went over to visit about six years ago, and rarely comes back. My parents have been to see her once, and she came back when Paps passed, but I need to visit her. At first she was helpful. But eventually she felt I was too needy after the whole divorce and baby.

She said it was time for her to put herself first. I get it. I'd made what I thought was my dream life and it consumed me. And then it fell apart, and it took over even more."

"I hope she's happy," was all Mack said, keeping it simple.

"My parents are going back for Christmas and they want me to come. I haven't decided. They also want me to date, so I don't really do much of what they want."

I wasn't sure why I admitted the last tidbit, but I did. Maybe as a safeguard, letting Mack know he was in the clear with me?

CHAPTER Fifteen

MACK

We pulled into the circle drive of the empty house and I wanted to turn around. I hated coming here. To me, it was nothing more than a house, but to Milly it was everything. So I'd kept it.

I had to come out today to grab an old deed my lawyer needed and saw it as a chance to see Frances—and apologize again.

"This is where you grew up?" she asked as we crossed the threshold.

"After my mom officially split. My dad sold the house they had together, and Milly had recently bought this one. I think she saw the whole disaster coming."

I allowed her a moment to take in the foyer, watching her strain her neck in an effort to look up at the crystal chandelier.

"It's from Germany. Milly might have loved her home cooking and hanging with the kids, but we were expected to respect her things."

Frances moved toward the wall and ran her palm over the surface. "Silk," she muttered.

I nodded at her back. She didn't need my confirmation.

"Did you have friends in the neighborhood?" This time, she turned to me.

"I did, and always brought friends home from college. It made it easier to have people around."

"And you don't want to live here? It's sitting here…empty."

"No."

My answer was firm, and she allowed us to move on without explanation.

"Come on, I'll give you a tour. We'll save the pièce de résistance for last."

"Paps would have called this place a *gem*. He loved visiting people's homes and helping them pick furniture. He'd say about so-and-so, they're living like the rich and famous…" She pulled her hair back into a tight ponytail, smoothing the sides, and took in every inch of the house.

"It wasn't all that it was cracked up to be. Sure, I had it all, but I didn't have a mom… I'm sorry to keep mentioning it. This place brings out the best and worst in me. That's why I don't live here. But I can't bring myself to sell it."

I showed her the office while I grabbed the paper I needed. She studied the photos on the wall. "Your aunt doesn't want it? Susie is her name, right?"

She ran a finger along the gold-edged frame, looking at my dad and Susie as kids.

"She probably does, but Milly had her affairs in order and this house was left to me. Susie got shares in the company and a lump sum, which her husband was very happy with. Her daughters got their college funds and jewelry."

"This is you?" Frances pointed at a little boy up in a chair at a party.

I nodded, walking closer. "Yes, actually Susie's wedding. The hora…"

"I know what it is—a celebratory dance at most Jewish occasions. They put the bride and groom up in chairs and dance all around them."

I watched her take in the photographs, a smile on her face and small furrow in her brow as she studied them.

"And the ring bearer got a turn too," she added with the sweetest smile.

I pointed to one of the men holding up the chair. "That's my dad."

"You don't look like him—" She caught herself, maybe realizing she was bringing up my mom without meaning to.

"I know. My curse when it came to him. Looking at me only reminded him of her. She was in the rest of the wedding pictures, so Milly took most of them down. Milly hated my mother with a passion."

"Milly was a strong woman. She raised her kids, endured all that with your grandfather, took you under her wing. Her legacy lives on."

"She was the brightest spot in my life." I ran a hand through my hair and looked at Frances. "I want to kiss you, but I'm not going to. Every time I give in to the need, I get spooked. It's true. I want you and more, Frances, and that's not something I ever saw for myself." I swallowed the pride lodged in my throat, and took her hand, giving it a squeeze.

Before she could respond, I led her out of the study, gave an abbreviated tour of the other rooms, save the kitchen, and headed to the armoire, hoping to get the goose chase out of the way...

"Here it is." I spoke gingerly, noting Frances's change in demeanor.

Her palm smoothed over the wood, rounding the edges and coming to the door, where she ran a finger along the brass handle. "I know this armoire. My grandparents had the same one." She spoke quietly, her words coming out one at a time. "It was in the hallway at my grandparents' house, and my grandmother called it her golden treasure chest. She kept sheets in the drawers and purses on the shelves. She also had a small jewelry box in the back corner."

"You can open it," was all I said, sensing Frances was in some sort of state, and not wanting to disturb her emotional response.

"My parents now use it for storage in the third bedroom, my old room. Mostly knickknacks," she rambled. "My mom said it doesn't go with the rest of her decor, but my dad insisted my grandfather loved the piece. They always ask if I want it, but I'm not sure it will fit in with my apartment."

With her slight hand and pale pink manicured nails, she opened the door, revealing a collection of Chanel bags and a whole shelf of perfume, mostly Rose's Lily. I hadn't touched a thing since Milly died. I left most of the house intact, paying someone to clean it as is.

Frances opened a perfume bottle and smelled it. "Maybe your aunt wants these?"

I laughed. "That's what you're going to suggest? Not that I'm a nutcase for not emptying it sooner? I did donate my grandmother's clothes to a nonprofit that helps women get back into the workforce."

"I just meant, the smell must remind you of Milly. Maybe Susie would like to wear it. You don't make it anymore."

"It's dated."

"It's beautiful," she said, rattling on about secrets and her parents. I couldn't make out what she was saying, but I heard her breath pick up. This whole experience had spiked my anxiety. I could only imagine what it had done to hers.

Pulling her to my chest, I said, "Breathe."

She took a deep inhale.

"Poor Frances. Take it easy. You're mumbling and stressing yourself out. I'm not one to ever think you should discuss something if you're not ready." I felt a bit of the tension bleed from her. "It doesn't surprise me they had matching armoires. Milly and James seemed to be in tune with one another no matter how much separation they had. And no, I don't need to give Susie a damn thing."

"Can I explore?" Frances asked me hesitantly, her hand ready to dive into the cabinet.

"Of course. Touch anything you want. You can even put on some perfume."

She immediately grabbed a bottle and spritzed some on her wrist.

"I was kidding…"

"I wasn't." She thumbed through the purses, oohing and aahing over a dark pink boucle one. "Sheila, who works in handbags, would die if she saw these."

"You can take them to show her."

"No, I could never. You have kept them for two decades in this cabinet. I'm not messing with a piece of your history." She was fiddling with a black quilted bag, opening it and looking inside. "They always have the nicest linings, Chanel…" She stopped in her tracks and said, "Oh, there's something in here."

Pulling out a folded stack of papers, she handed them to me.

Her hand shook and my mind raced.

"Is that what I think it is?" Frances asked me, the two of us communicating in a way I didn't believe possible.

I nodded, whispering, "Letters."

Frances waited patiently, and I wished I'd gone ahead and kissed her earlier, delaying this moment.

I cleared my throat and read the top page.

My Dearest James…

You're no longer mine. My Jimmy.

You probably won't even see this letter. I'm writing it more as a reminder to myself.

Today, I got myself all dressed and put my grandson, Mackenzie, in the car, and had the driver bring us to your store.

It's a lovely store. Big, busy, and full of items I'd choose.

It's Christmastime, and Santa was there for young families to visit. What a great idea! I knew you would be successful.

There hasn't been a day I haven't thought about you.

I've been married for a long time, but this still holds true. My husband is a good man, a hard worker, and we made a life. But I can't help but think what life with you would have been like.

I wanted to see you happy. Seeing you help a customer, smiling and thriving, was what I needed. Your wife came to call you away, and she looks like a nice person with kind eyes, and I decided it was lucky you didn't see me. I'm sure your family is very happy.

I didn't want to linger and not buy something or take up a salesperson's time for nothing, so I purchased an armoire. It will look beautiful in my house.

My grandson, Mackenzie, lives with me now. His mom left him, and he'll never be the same.

My heart dropped to my feet at this statement, and Frances grabbed my hand and squeezed tight.

"I'm fine," I muttered. I didn't know if it was for me or her or Milly or who…

I hope one day he finds a love like we had, and no one tears him away. He deserves it.

Merry Christmas,
Forever your Rosie

My throat clogged toward the end, my words coming out sounding like a frog was lodged in my vocal cords.

When I started to pull out the second letter, Frances touched my hand and said, "Let's save it for another time. That was a lot to digest."

She looked into my eyes, her expression soft and comforting, like a blanket tucking in my tired, aching heart.

Stealing the letters from me with her free hand, she said, "It's my turn to say I'm sorry. I didn't realize how much this would be for you.

The internet makes you out to be a badass, and for some reason I thought this would be a quick thing. And that you would just tell me what you knew, or I don't know. But you're hurt…"

I pulled a rambling Frances into my chest, and whispered, "Shh."

I kissed the top of her head, my mouth brushing against her soft hair. I breathed her in; she smelled like peaches and mango. I wanted to hold her tighter, feel her closer as the two of us stood in between the open doors of the armoire. More like a Pandora's box, but I didn't want to add any more pain to the woman in my arms.

"It's true, I'm sorry." Her mouth tickled my chest while she spoke, and I wrapped her small body tighter.

I didn't want to look at her while I spoke. "My mom is a bad subject. I spent most of my childhood wishing she would come back. Then, I've spent the great majority of my adult life putting her away on a high shelf. Keeping her out of my story, away from my business and in the back recesses of my mind, has been my mission. She's the one who hurt me. Clearly Milly knew it. I don't like others to be privy to it because they can take advantage of it. But that's not you. You wouldn't do that. I've known that since the day you hijacked my soul at the mall…"

I felt her tilt her head back and look up at me. "I did not hijack your soul."

My lips met the top of her head again. "You did. You and your kickboxing moves…"

"I'm falling for you," she blurted out. "Shit!" She stole away from my grasp. "I didn't mean to put that out there."

I strode toward her, wanting her back in my arms.

"I never wanted to fall for anyone. I'm thirty-eight…too old for crushes and *like*-liking someone, you know? I see men all day and I never fall for anyone. Working with men in my safe place. I am unemotional when it comes to your sex—ugh! This is not coming out right. Working with men has been a way for me to keep up boundaries. I don't like your kind!"

This had me laughing. "Well, you just said you are falling for me, so I disagree." I wrangled her back into my arms. "Frankie..." I said against her forehead.

"Not Frances?"

"Frances, beautiful Frances," I corrected myself. "I said earlier all I want to do is kiss you, but I don't want to run the other way from you. I want to race toward you. But Milly was right, I'm broken in certain ways. More than most, I recognize. Being with you shows me that life doesn't have to be like it was with my parents...or my grandparents. I just am trying to slow the process because I want to do things right... or how they feel right."

"Mack." My name was a breath or a whisper. "Kiss me."

I couldn't say no to Frances, so I did as I was told. My mouth melted into hers, the tension rising quickly. Her lips parted so our tongues could meet and I felt like I breathed in as she exhaled out.

I was in trouble. I'd spent decades crafting industrial-strength walls around my heart, while not forgiving myself for abandoning what Milly wanted. Now, when I was closer to fifty than forty, my grandmother was taking the reins. Frances Burns was not going anywhere, and I wasn't sure I wanted her to go anymore.

With the letters still in one hand, the other palm sliding up and down my back, she said, "Let's get out of here."

"And forget the house tour?"

"Screw the tour," she said, and we did.

CHAPTER Sixteen

FRANKIE

"Do you have them in dark gray too?"

I looked up from my iPad and said, "Of course. Navy and black like you're buying. Dark gray, a lighter gray, and taupe. A lighter taupe."

Cam Hawkins, another longtime customer of mine, said, "I'll take them all. When they come in I will have them fitted and shipped to my condo in Aspen for the winter."

I nodded, making notes on my iPad. Without the tablet, I was a goner. The tiny computer kept all my client records and orders. "You should add a few cashmere sweaters for the evenings. Maybe with jeans."

Cam nodded and said, "You're right. If I take an evening meeting, it makes me more approachable."

"Bingo!" I agreed, knowing Cam and his business well. "Let me pull a few darker-wash jeans and a sweater."

Cam was already flipping through a table of socks and giving me a thumbs-up.

As I went to look for a particular pair of jeans, I thought why not someone like Cam for me? Wealthy, smart, owned a venture capital fund, and spent three months a year in Aspen, skiing and meeting with techies. I knew for a fact that he found a ton of business opportunities on these trips—while having an equal amount of fun—because I outfitted him every year. He came in every August before heading to Europe for a major shopping haul, having everything fitted when he returned from Italy or Spain or wherever he went, and then shipped to Aspen in time for his December arrival.

Cam wasn't complicated. Sure, he had a significant other, but I worked with hundreds of Cams. Instead I'd gone and admitted to liking the world's least eligible bachelor. A man who'd had commitment issues long before I sent him further into a tailspin.

My phone dinged as I grabbed a pair of Paige jeans, and I took a quick peek. Speaking of the devil, Mackenzie Miller was texting me.

Still on for dinner later? How is the club? Perfect night to eat on the roof...

Like I said, Mack was in a tailspin. Usually commanding and domineering in his requests, he was asking me if we were still on. There was an air of hesitancy in all of his interactions since we returned from Westchester a few days ago. He couched his actions in wanting to go about things the right way, but I chalked it up to a protective way.

I answered him quickly and went back to Cam.

Yes. 8? I'm busy at work today. I can meet you there.

No matter what, I had to keep my work strong. It was the only steady facet of my life.

He sent a thumbs-up emoji and *See you then*. He didn't mention the newly found letters that were still in my possession, or much of what happened.

"Here you go," I told Cam, handing him the jeans. "These will be perfect." I'd found a pale blue cashmere sweater too and told him, "Try this for size. I can get any color, really."

"Before I forget, I need a pair of lug-sole shoes to walk around the lodge in." He ran a hand through his brown hair, a large Rolex catching the light.

It only made me think of Mack and his beautiful face and damaged heart. Shaking the thought away, I told Cam I had just the pair and went off to grab them.

He loved them, took the brown ones and had me order black with the rest of the items I was ordering.

"I'll be back from Italy mid-September, and then we'll get it all set to ship."

"Of course. Have fun."

"Any summer travels for you?

Cam had asked only to be polite, but it made me think. I hadn't been on a vacation in a while. *Maybe I should take a breather...* "Not yet, but I shall see," I told him.

"I hope you do. Thanks for everything, Frankie," he said and was off.

The rest of the day was a flurry of wedding clients, and it was close to seven when I had a moment to fix my makeup and go to the bathroom.

On my way out, I cruised through the cosmetics section, stopping at the Silky counter. We didn't carry as big of a selection as the Silky stores, but they had a presence—the latest glittery body lotion and lip gloss collections next to a few bottles of perfume. There was a new scent called Sun. I picked it up and smelled. It was all daisy and marigolds, mixed with a dewy rain scent. I loved it and put a spritz on, thinking I should buy a bottle before making my way outside.

It was beautiful out, the humidity strangely low for August, and I decided to walk a few blocks before ordering a rideshare. Allowing the fresh air to wash over me, I headed west, the sun setting in front of me.

What am I doing? I asked myself. I couldn't shake the thought as I made my way to Eighth and pulled up the app for the car.

I hadn't resolved a thing by the time I arrived at Mack's club and strode into the lobby where he waited for me, in dark jeans like I'd sold Cam and a white dress shirt rolled up at the sleeves. If luscious and unachievable were a scent, it would be called *Mack*.

"Hi," he whispered, pulling me in for a hug.

"Hey," I found myself responding. "You okay?" I couldn't help myself; I was strangely attracted to men who would destroy me. That was the only answer I could come up with.

"I'm good now," he said for only me, his hand coming to my lower back as he guided me toward the elevators.

How could something feel incredibly right and wrong at the same time?

"Mr. Miller, right this way," someone said as soon as we exited the elevator.

We were escorted to a table toward the back of the roof, a view of the pool and sunset looming in front of us.

"Corey called and set everything up," Mack said as we sat. "Wish I could take credit, but I had a sales meeting I couldn't ditch."

I nodded as though we hadn't shared this extremely emotional and physical moment the weekend prior.

Mack spoke first. "Let's get a drink."

"Let's. I could use one." Truer words had never been spoken.

Mack signaled for the server and ordered a mule for himself after asking me what I wanted.

"White, something crisp," I requested.

"Thank you for coming. I know it's been awkward, but texting and calling felt like the wrong way to discuss what is happening."

"Happening?" I crossed my legs under the table, all sorts of tension crackling between us.

"I guess it's solely about me. My reaction to the new letters, my feelings for you, all of this. Fuck, Frances, you turn me into a bumbling idiot."

He leaned forward, staring me down with dark eyes swirling with a kaleidoscope of emotions. Need, confusion, and lust were what I felt the strongest.

He went on. "I don't know what to say, or where to start… This doesn't come naturally to me."

"How about, 'How was your day?'"

I suggested the question as our drinks arrived, so with his copper mug in hand, he said, "How was your day?"

"It was good…mostly the norm…my customers needing me, and I like that. It's predictable, and they appreciate me in a way I crave, I guess. At the end of the day, I love it because it's a feel-good transaction."

"None of your customers give you a hard time?"

I felt my head shaking and took a sip of my wine. "No. Maybe in the beginning, but not now. I'm respected and know what they need, and I only work with a certain level of customer. Someone like yourself, who has money to burn and needs to look on top of his game, all the time."

"Are you soliciting my business?" He raised an eyebrow. "Was that your intention?"

The twinkle in his left eye let me know he was joking, but I played along. "No, my book is full and I don't have time for your demands."

He brought a hand to his heart. "That wounds me."

Together, we laughed and the mood reset to something between easy and perfect. Conversation flowed as we shared a cheeseburger and fries. Mack dipped a fry in ketchup and fed it to me. The way he stared as I ate it gave me chills.

"Wait!" I was halfway through the fry when I spoke.

Mack raised an eyebrow, and I quickly finished chewing.

"Can you eat a cheeseburger? I feel bad—I suggested it and now you ate it…"

He reached across the table and took my hand. "I don't keep kosher. Milly did when she grew up and also after marrying my grandpa. But when they got older, she didn't follow it when she was out of the house. She would take me for cheeseburgers at the local diner, 'because if you're going to eat out, it better be for something good' she'd say."

"I love the way you smile when you talk about Milly. It's clear she was such a bright spot in your life."

I felt his fingers tighten on mine. "She was the only bright spot for a long time, and now I've let her down."

Taking another sip of my wine, I dared to ask, "Do you want to see the second letter?"

"Did you read it?"

I nodded.

"Did she mention my sad state of affairs again?"

Thankfully, I was able to say, "No."

With our hands still tangled on the table, I felt his foot slide my way and touch my ankle. They were intimate gestures among two people, both with cracks in their past and fears twisted with misconceptions when it came to love. But it was a start. A beginning to what might be a new middle for us both.

"How about you tell me? Give me the condensed version."

He took his hand away for a moment to take a chug of his drink, quickly returning it to my already painfully lonesome fingers.

"Well, it started with her new usual. 'My Dearest James.' She wrote the same explanation of him not being her Jimmy anymore, and then went on to elaborate on how him not being hers was her biggest regret." I stopped and took a long breath, dragging in air and courage before I said the next part. "The letter appears to be written on the day she was diagnosed. She mentioned just leaving the doctor and not knowing what to do other than write to her Jimmy, like she did during the year they were falling in love. Writing letters had become her way of coping, she explained. She had a separate line for not having the heart to tell her *Dear Mackenzie.*" I whispered the last part.

He nodded. "I never knew about the cancer until after she died."

My heart ached for the many burdens Mack toted around, but I didn't have time to tell him because he said, "Go on."

"She detailed how you had done so well in school and how you were making strides in the industry and becoming the man she always knew you would be. She went on to say that you would make a dedicated husband and father one day like she was sure my Paps was."

He squeezed his eyes shut. I wasn't sure what he needed from me—comforting, more information, or for me to plain shut up.

"Go on," he repeated.

It was clear he wanted me to finish. I thought about lying and saying that was it, but he'd see the letter eventually. After all, they were his. "She explained how she knew my Paps would never see the letter, and how she had not been brave enough to reach out since the day at the store. But that writing down about her dying and telling him, made it feel real…" It all came flying out, jumbled, and without my taking a breath.

He motioned to continue with his hand.

"She assured him she'd had love and caring in her life, and her children went on to do as much as any mom would wish. Susie being the one who went on to live a fuller life, marry and have many kids, probably because her life began further away from Milly's heartache. She told him about the regret she felt over your dad being born so close to her being ripped away from the love of her life. Then it was mostly a lot of gushy stuff. She'd die always loving her Jimmy and would be watching from above."

"Jeez," Mack breathed out. "I had no idea she harbored something like this. At least I'm successful and rich and the company is threefold what it was…because I'm certainly not a husband or father."

"*Yet.* Shit, I didn't mean to say that. I wasn't being presumptuous—" In an instant, the frivolity of sharing a burger was long forgotten.

He didn't speak to my ridiculous statement. He simply said, "Let's get out of here."

CHAPTER Seventeen

MACK

*I*t felt heavy, and that wasn't what I wanted. I didn't want to be a disappointment to Milly—and I wanted to impress Frances with my charm and my ability to be a better man. Sitting there talking about my dead grandmother's letter to her long-lost love wasn't accomplishing either.

"Do you have to work tomorrow?" I asked her.

"I have some late afternoon appointments," Frances explained as we rode down in the elevator and walked outside in the Meatpacking District.

The city was still bustling and people walked in all kinds of directions around us.

"I want to take the morning off… Want to ride out to the Hamptons and wake up by the beach?"

It was presumptuous of me to want to spend the night together; we never had.

"I don't have any of my stuff…" She looked around her as if her belongings would materialize.

"I can have Alex grab us and we can swing by your place."

She swiped her hand behind her and let her ponytail down, shaking her head.

Impulse took over and I gathered her close and kissed her right there on the street corner for the world to see. *Mackenzie Miller is a new man…*

"It's late," she mumbled.

"We can sleep in, order breakfast or whatever, walk on the beach, and Alex can bring us back in time for you to work."

"And what about you?"

"That's Corey's problem."

"He is going to hate me."

I kissed her again, our mouths dancing against one another. Pulling back, I asked, "Is that a yes?"

"Okay. If it saves your place from the dust bunnies, I'm in," she said with a smile, and I pulled out my phone.

Alex grumbled a bit until I added I'd be bringing Frances, and all of a sudden he was on board with the idea.

*W*ith Frances asleep on my shoulder, we pulled into the driveway around a quarter after midnight. With a soft kiss to her forehead I woke her, and she looked up as if she wasn't exhausted. I helped her out of the car, grabbing her duffel, and we walked to the front door.

"What about Alex?"

"He will stay in the pool house," I told her.

My house might be a funky bungalow, but it was the separate quarters in the back that had sold it to me.

Inside the house, Frances slipped off her shoes, her pink toes matching the soft hue on the walls. "It's so beachy here," she said. "So different than your apartment. I like it."

"I always felt like it had a few touches of Milly's place."

"It does."

This time it was Frances who stood on her tiptoes and kissed me, her duffel falling at our feet. We stayed that way for a while in the hallway until our bodies were grinding and moving along one another, seeking friction.

"Does it feel too fast?" I didn't want to push her, but my lower half was urgent to get involved with Frances's entire being.

"No. It's been a little rocky, but this feels right," she told me, and I lifted her up immediately.

Not making it farther than the kitchen, I set her on the counter and continued to kiss her while my hand worked its way around the back of her pencil skirt, unzipping the fabric. "Lift," I told her, and she did as she was told, her ass rising off the quartz.

I shimmied the skirt off, and before doing what I wanted, I lifted her blouse off. A button popped yet she didn't seem to mind. My mouth came to hers again before I yanked back and took her in. In a mint green satin bra and white lace panties, she was perfection.

"Frances, I want to devour you."

She giggled. "That's quite the line to use in the kitchen…"

"I don't give a fuck if you laugh because you're about to be screaming."

Before she could respond, I grabbed a cushion from the chair and tossed it on the floor, coming down on my knees and tugging her panties to the side.

I was fully clothed, and sweat beaded on my back as I swept my tongue along her most delicate parts, her moan more luscious than I imagined. Her growl ghosting every nerve in my body, I couldn't get enough of her—every sensation, sound, taste, smell…

I went to work, noting when Frances tossed her head back. With one eye on her chest heaving up and down, her bra barely containing her and her body rippling at every touch of my tongue, I took her almost there and then backed her down.

"I've fucking died," I told her.

"Mack," she begged.

"You have been bossing me around since we met. Not today, Feisty Frankie."

Being so close to the ocean, the air was already damp. But with every ooh and aah, the room filled with a heady sensation.

"Please, Mack," Frances repeated, and I capitulated, picking up speed, applying pressure where I noticed she was most sensitive.

I inhaled every shiver and sensation from her, allowing her to ride the wave, my mouth never letting up. When her hand squeezed my hair and she pulled me up for a kiss, I was smitten all over again with her. With her taste on my tongue, we kissed, and she started pulling off my shirt, running her palms down my back and squeezing my ass through my jeans.

"This can't be comfortable," she said, looking down at my pants-covered length.

"I don't want to do anything you don't want...but I need you with every cell in my fucking body, Frances. I don't even know how we got to this place, but we are here. And I never want to leave."

"Have me—I have an IUD," Frances whispered, urgent with desire and practical in sharing important information.

We weren't kids. We knew what we wanted and we were going to take a taste of it.

Frances squirmed to bring our bodies closer, if possible. She didn't echo my sentiment on never wanting this to end, but I was already unzipping my pants and shoving them off, along with the shoes on my feet, and pushing her back on the counter. My chest pounded as my hand ran up Frances's soft abdomen, and I could feel her own heart beating a furious rhythm close to mine as I positioned myself to enter her.

"We can use the bed later," was all I said. I couldn't even wait in this moment—the kitchen felt like the only place to savor the delicacy known as Frances.

"Mack." My name was once again a whimper on Frances's breath, and I couldn't help but indulge our desires, slipping inside her slowly, picking up speed as my palm traversed every inch of her skin.

She equally explored my chest and back as I guided myself in and out of her. Her breath picked up and tiny ripples spread through her body. She clenched me as she started to go off again, and I was only moments behind.

"Shit, that could have been a lot more romantic," I mumbled while spread over Frances on my kitchen counter, my weight held up by my forearm and my free hand running through her hair.

"It was perfect, but the kitchen is definitely going to need to be sanitized. Hope the cleaning crew comes tomorrow."

This woman. She had a way of making every moment the perfect balance of emotions.

The next morning, I woke in a tangle of blond hair and small limbs. I noted to myself that Frances slept as feistily as she lived. I spent a beat or two watching her wake up before whispering, "Hi."

We'd fallen asleep after a second round in the sheets and a warm shower that followed.

"This is awkward," the beautiful woman in my bed mumbled.

"You don't do this often?" I couldn't help but tease and fish for an answer at the same time.

"You know I don't." Her voice still raspy with sleep had me ready for more of whatever she was willing to give.

Gathering her close, I whispered, "Probably because they're afraid you'll kickbox them to death."

"Very funny…and it's distracting from how strange this whole scenario is. I mean, how many times have you ditched me? And here I am, in bed with you."

I brought my hand to her cheek and smoothed my palm over her skin, making my way to her hair, gliding my fingers through her soft locks. It was as sincere a moment as I'd ever had, but I wasn't sure how to put it into words. "I've had a lot of experiences in life. Privilege is practically my middle name—"

She interrupted. "Don't. You work hard. You built most of what you have," she insisted, and it was pure Frances.

"Do you always have to prove a point? Your point?"

"I do…and you grew your company."

Pinching her cheek, I admitted, "I did, but that doesn't mean I haven't lived a good life. I've never wanted for anything, other than my mom. Which I never say to anyone. When I got over her, I decided doing what I wanted, working, playing, was enough. Then, you came along. I don't know how but you made me want something I'd tabled for myself. Now here you are. And yes, I have left you at key moments. My own pride got in the way."

"Well, I just meant that one minute we were at dinner, and the next in the Hamptons in a bed…"

"Well, on a kitchen counter first," I clarified.

"Ha. Now move. I have morning breath."

"I don't care," I said, and I didn't. I hoped she truly understood this was awkward for me too. Not the "waking up in the Hamptons with someone" but caring for another person.

Although, for the record, it wasn't often that I woke next to a woman.

"Let me brush my teeth. One minute," Frances said while wiggling out of my arms.

She would not be denied and slithered out from the bed. I decided to do the same, and hurried to brush my teeth if it meant getting back in between the sheets with Frances.

While Corey was shocked, I'd called off the morning. I imagined him doing some kind of Millsy dance in excitement over it.

Which was exactly what he was doing that afternoon when I walked into the office, armored in a suit and needing a strong cup of coffee before my afternoon of shitty tasks.

I found Corey in my office, whistling "Here Comes the Bride," and asked him, "Do you always prance around my office when I'm out, planning imaginary weddings?"

He stopped mid-track and held his hands up in the air, declaring, "Guilty!"

"Okay, let's get to work. I need to talk to the supplier for the new bottles for the new scent. They were having some sort of shipping issue."

Corey nodded and started walking out toward his desk before turning and asking, "How was the night?"

"Get that smirk off your face, Corey," I said while laughing. He feigned hurt and I finally gave in. "Fucking great. Now get them on the phone. I need to solve this issue and then I have to run out for a bit."

After sorting the packaging issues and negotiating a better price, I checked my email and stood up to go. I had a visit to make, and I'd grab a coffee on the way. There was something on the edges of my mind, a piece of the puzzle that I'd been trying to jam into the wrong slot.

Alex drove me to the Upper East Side and pulled over at a little local coffee shop a block away from where I was heading. I went in, grabbed two coffees, and walked the rest of the way to my destination. The doorman quickly opened the door for me, knowing who I was, and buzzed me up without calling. Which was how I surprised my dear aunt Susie at her apartment. I knew she'd be home because it was a Thursday in August. Tomorrow morning she'd dash to the Hamptons like everyone else in her world.

"Mack?"

"Here, I brought you a coffee." I handed off one of the disposable cups and took a long slug from the other while walking inside her gaudy apartment.

"What are you doing here? I mean, it's nice to see you, but unexpected." She smoothed her dyed-black hair behind her ear, showing off her Botoxed cheek. "Did you want to talk about the potential business arrangement with Tom? We could still arrange a meeting with Traci, the woman I told you about. I understand not wanting to do it over the Jewish New Year, but Tom's not here. Obviously."

"No." I spoke firmly, walking farther into the apartment, saying hello to the housekeeper, who was staring at me as if I was the only person to ever barge in there. I probably was.

"I was getting ready to leave in the morning. The kids are all coming out to the beach place for the weekend."

I nodded. "I don't really care."

Standing in front of the grand piano that no one played, she asked, "What are you upset about, then?"

I faced her and asked what I wanted to know. "Do you ever go out to Westchester?" Something about the house and my chat with Frances had started the thoughts churning in my mind. The last twenty-four hours an onslaught of questions had clouded my brain.

"No, it's not my place to go. It's yours—remember?"

"You grew up there," I countered.

"So did you. More recently than me."

"You have history there. So why is it Milly left me the house, and the business mostly became mine, and you got a lump sum and were left out of the family legacy? That's what I need to know, Susie. I'm missing something here. Milly wanted you out of Silky…she'd told my dad as much."

I downed some more coffee, no longer needing the caffeine jolt but my throat was dry with anticipation. My aunt stood there, cup in hand, looking at me with wide eyes.

"Do tell," I encouraged her. "I'm not leaving until you answer."

"Do you want to sit?" She motioned to the couch behind me.

"No. Talk, Susie. I'd ask my dad but he's not here. And let's face it, he lived in some alternate reality. He was never reliable…for anything."

She nodded. "We all felt bad about that. Your mom, she ruined him. Milly took on the burden but it wasn't her fault."

"You don't think I know that? If you hadn't noticed, I'm a grown-ass man. I know exactly what my mom did. All too well. I certainly don't need to be babied or talked down to. Tell me what I'm missing."

"Milly wanted it this way," was all she said. She kept her tone even and her facial expressions schooled.

"Why would she want her only daughter out of her family legacy?"

"I meant she wanted me to keep quiet and treat you with care. You were her baby, the light of her life, and the one she wanted to have happiness. She was different with you. Don't you get that?"

Clearing growing emotion from my throat, I asked, "What are you getting at? I was a burden. Yeah, Milly loved me, but she'd raised her kids and spent my lifetime annoyed with my mother for not taking care of me."

Susie shook her head. "You were her second chance, the one she was going to launch into the world for all things good and golden. Silky was ripe for expansion, and the world was a different place when it came to love and living."

I stared at my aunt—in a flash it became clear she knew about Jimmy Burns. I waited patiently for her to cop to it and explain how she fit into the story.

She turned away from me for a quick second. When she swiveled back, she spoke softly. "I knew something I shouldn't, and Milly never wanted me to discuss it. But I still did something I shouldn't have… and Milly made sure I would never do it again. She took the house away from me, drew up the terms for my shares of Silky and passed them on to your dad for future use, and made it impossible for me to ever touch your greatness. If I did, she promised to dissolve any future college accounts for imaginary children I'd have at that point."

"What?" I growled the question, needing to know why I didn't know any of this, and how it potentially affected Frances.

Fuck, Frances, this would blow back on her. Another way I could hurt her. Susie didn't know who Frances was or that she was even in my life. But with my falling harder for Frances, I could inadvertently serve her up into Susie's warped world.

"You knew what? And did what? Look, Susie, I'm missing work and I need you to get on with it. I don't need your niceties, only your explanation." I growled her name, and lasered my eyes on her.

She looked away again before staring me back dead-on. With her elbow on the piano, she started to speak. "It was around the time I got pregnant. I'd gone out to see Milly. You were just a kid, playing with some fancy building set in the playroom. Milly wanted to see me and make sure I was taking care of myself. You know Milly. She'd made some homemade vegetable soup and watched me eat a bowl. Truthfully, I had a ball to attend and wanted to borrow one of Milly's Chanel bags…so I made the trek out to see her."

I nodded. Now I knew where this started. And I feared where it ended. "You found the letter?" I blurted out the question, already knowing the answer.

It must have been the first one, not the second one detailing Milly's illness, because that would have been added much later. I didn't need to hear any more pointless details from Susie but remained a captive audience.

"I did read it, but I didn't tell Milly. I put it back where it was and took a different bag so she would think nothing of it."

"Then what?" I started to pace Susie's cream-colored area rug.

"I decided to find Jimmy Burns. We all knew there was a sadness to Milly, and with Dad gone for so long already, I was going to be the one to fix it. In my mind, it would win me points with Milly. So, I hired someone to locate potential Jimmy Burnses, and when I discovered the right one, I went to see him. Took a car service out to Long Island, and

I told him your grandma still loved him and wrote imaginary letters to him, and he needed to reach out to her. He was a nice man. Definitely had a twinkle in his eye when he heard Milly's name. 'My Rosie'— he murmured it, but I caught it. Anyway, he showed me pictures of his family and said it wasn't possible. He was loyal to the woman he married despite his heart still carrying feelings for Rosie. He wished me well, said to tell Rosie he sent his best, and led me out."

"So he wouldn't see Milly? Or call? Or anything?" I couldn't help but think how this would crush Frances. "How did she know you went to see him?"

"*He called.* Reached out to Milly. It was only once, but it was enough as far as Milly was concerned. He said he was sorry about my dad, your grandfather, passing and that I'd gone to see him and how great it was to meet me. He emphasized that I was a lovely young woman, but he couldn't be a part of Milly's life. She was irate with me, inviting Jimmy back into her world when her own parents had banished him. I'd never once seen Milly cry except for when she quickly turned away from me. A tear had started to form in her eye when she spoke about her parents. After composing herself, she explained to me she wasn't allowed to date Jimmy. She'd been ripped away from him and sent to her cousins for a short while before being married off to Harold."

Filing away every fact, I shook my head, not wanting to let on how much I already knew.

"Did you know any of this?" Susie stared at me. "You and your happiness were the whole reason Milly went crazy on me. This story was supposed to die with her. And here you are, knowing about the letter. I assume you found it? Is that all? Was there more?"

Clearing my throat, I lied. "I don't know much. I found the letter. And there was a second one written, closer to the time Milly passed. I assume you don't know about that one?"

"No." Susie crossed her arms in front of her.

"I put a bunch of stuff together in my mind, figuring this Jimmy was an ex, one she was presumably ripped away from…"

"Her parents absolutely forbade it. When she told me, she said it was the darkest time in her life. She was also not surprised Jimmy wouldn't see her. 'He's a good man,' she'd said. 'The best, and I'd expect nothing less from him than to be loyal.'"

"Sounds like she went into a lot of detail with you? To then turn around and hold it against you?"

"It was a weak moment on her part. That's all I can chalk it up to."

I still couldn't believe Jimmy called Milly, and wondered if I should share that with Frances. I knew better than to mention Frances to Susie now. Susie would make assumptions about status and relationships, just like she had when it came to Milly. Granted, her heart might have been in the right place with Jimmy, but her judgment was off when it came to society.

But would Frances stay away from Susie? She was the type of woman who left no stone unturned. If she wasn't satisfied with our findings, she might seek out Susie.

"After speaking the truth, Milly lost her mind. Told me it was her life, her story, her mistakes, and not mine to barge in and get involved. She spewed hatred over me visiting Jimmy. I was a foolish daughter, one who meddled in business that wasn't hers. But I thought it was a sweet idea at the time."

That, I couldn't disagree with. But this wasn't the time for my opinions.

Susie strode to the other side of the piano, wringing her hands. "Milly said it was my fault he called and opened old wounds. For him and her, she made note. Then she stressed how she'd spent decades packing Jimmy away, and I was never to speak his name again. Not to your dad or you. She said you were going to live your life without knowing of any more pain and suffering. And I was going to feel the hurt of stepping out of line."

Susie didn't cry or get emotional over the spat with Milly. She spit her words out laced with venom.

"She was protective of me." It was a thoughtless thing to say, but in the moment I still didn't want to divulge how much I knew, or how, or why. Let alone the other letters and meeting Connie. Why? Because all roads went back to Frances.

"Well, she was not protective of me. She made sure I was cut out of her life in many ways, not to mention the future of the family was all safeguarded for you."

"I didn't do that."

"I know, but it's hard not to resent you. The golden child with the clean slate, free from Milly's past, forging into the future."

"You're the one who dredged her past up."

"Well, now you know, so you can leave," was all she said, and I was happy to do as I was told.

"I sure can. And in case you still wondered, I won't be joining you for the Jewish holiday. None of this is my doing, Susie, and I can't be blamed for others' actions."

I couldn't be mad at Milly for protecting me and not wanting me to know the sad details of her past, but I could be mad at Susie for reopening old wounds for the only steady person in my life, whether it was born in a good place or not. Susie hurt Milly, and my love for my grandmother couldn't handle the notion of that.

CHAPTER Eighteen

FRANKIE

Big plans for Labor Day weekend?

Mack sent the text on his way home from Paris. He'd been gone for a few days, meeting with various lily oil suppliers. His factory was experiencing a shortage, and with the rollout of a new scent they couldn't afford to be low. He'd explained this all over a quick brunch last week. We'd gone for a run together—which was awkward since running had always been a therapeutic time for me, not social—and then we'd hit up a nearby café, all sweaty and stinky.

I have a client tomo at noon, and then I'm off all weekend. Might binge a TV series.

I wasn't fishing for an invite or a plan. Other than our running and brunch date, I hadn't seen Mack. Well, he did leave for Paris that Monday, but he hadn't offered to go out Saturday night or Sunday and didn't seem inclined to jump into bed again. Since I wasn't twenty-five,

I didn't mention any of this to Rachel or my sister when she'd called a few days ago. In fact, I didn't mention much to Ashley, other than I was thinking about seeing Mom and Dad. She was still hopelessly in love, with no plans to return to the States. And to be honest, it didn't seem like she cared about much other than herself.

As for me, I couldn't stop thinking about the deep furrow in Mack's brow. It felt as if there was an extra worry on his plate. He didn't share, and I didn't ask.

Any chance you'd binge the show with me? In the Hamptons?

I gulped my coffee and stared at the phone, thinking I might need to work on reconciling when a man was busy with work and not blowing me off. Clearly, it was a byproduct of Jeremy deserting me. I needed to make quick work of ditching the habit.

Maybe. What do you think of the British monarchy?

Nothing better...pick you up at 4 tomo?

Did this mean he'd resolved whatever was bothering him, or he planned to share it with me? There was no escaping that I wanted to see the man, so I replied *yes* and padded to my closet to see what I should pack. Later that night, I got a text from Corey asking me for a grocery list, stressing I didn't have to cook, but if I wanted to, send him the ingredients.

Deciding on brunch foods, grilled fish with veggies, and an apple pie, I kept my order small.

That's nothing, Corey noted.

I didn't respond. Rather, I met with my client, got them fitted with a suit for a fall wedding they were attending and several casual looks for an upcoming trip of theirs, and went straight home to get ready for Mack.

"Want to go for a swim?" Mack asked, an inviting smirk on his face.

"What?" I asked, inserting a coquettish lilt to my tone.

Two could play this flirting game.

It was after we'd eaten Italian takeout and caught up on the week, and the need and sexual tension between us was climbing. Mack had secured a new supplier for lily oil and explained a bit on how it was extracted from the flower. Which reminded me that I'd been wanting to tell him something about the bloom, but apparently we'd moved on to new topics.

"A swim?" Mack repeated himself.

I cut to the chase. "A naked swim?"

"It could be arranged…"

"Hmmm…I hadn't thought about skinny-dipping. I did bring a swimsuit."

Mack leaned closer, running his hand behind my hair, his palm settling at the nape of my neck, and kissed me. It was closed-mouth, soft, and tender. Our lips lingered for a while until Mack pulled back.

"Missed you," he said as though this was commonplace.

"I don't know what to say. My life was chugging along before you, and now it's racing to places unknown."

"Like the pool?"

His palm caressed my cheek. He might have been teasing with his words, but his eyes showed me that he got me. He understood my apprehension. Maybe he matched it in spades, but the pool and Mack naked sounded better than a serious chat.

"To the pool." I stood, untying my dress at the shoulder and letting it fall to the patio. I stood in front of him in my lace thong and matching bra.

He stared for a beat, and then stood and made haste with his own clothes. "You still take new clients?" Mack asked, slipping his hand in his boxer briefs and shoving them down.

Earlier, I'd mentioned a new client at work. "Maybe. Depends on who refers them."

Mack got close, invading my space, sliding my bra strap off one shoulder, leaning in and running his tongue along my clavicle. "What if I referred myself?"

He ran his tongue back up my neck, his lips meeting my mouth, and we stopped talking. His hand slid down my back and into the waistband of my thong, shoving it down. I helped, kicking off my flip-flop and lifting my leg out of the small panties. He unclasped my bra and it met the pile of clothes on the ground before he took my hand and led me to the pool.

Mack's eyes seared into me as I traversed the steps into the water, grateful for it being warm and covering my belly. I was old enough to know not to mention those types of things in mixed company. I was never fishing for compliments, but it came off insincere and immature so I kept my negative thoughts at bay, locking them away.

The water rippled behind me, and then Mack was everywhere— behind me, sliding in front of me, walking me toward the wall, mouth on me as my legs came around his waist.

Gone was the worry over what was bothering him. We'd found out as much as we could on Paps, and there was nothing I could do to change his ending. I could have a few magnificent moments of my own with this man who'd come to mean something to me, so I did.

We kissed, the night sky darkening, the quiet murmur of the water, an occasional hum of a bird or insect littering the air, and our breaths swirling.

"I've never wanted to get back to someone when I was away. I only ever returned to Corey and my apartment."

My hand slid up his damp back and I squeezed his shoulder blade. "I've never missed anyone," I admitted.

We spoke through broken kisses and ragged moans. I felt Mack's fingers tickle down my side, finding their way to my heat. Right there, in the pool, naked for anyone to see—not really, he had a very private backyard—Mack brought me to climax so quickly, I was a goner.

I'd never hit the crescendo so fast or furious, and I was ready for all of Mack. "Please," I mumbled.

"You don't have to beg. I'm here for your taking," Mack told me, sucking on my earlobe and using a hand to guide himself inside me.

It was a heady sensation, the added friction of the water, our slapping sounds against the still evening…

"Now you know why I wanted to get the groceries. No interruptions," Mack uttered as he drove faster.

I felt myself building again, and like he knew, Mack slowed.

I think his name came out like a growl, and he responded with, "Patience, Feisty Frankie."

I lightly bit into his shoulder as he took his time…

"Savoring you," he said with his hand behind me, protecting my back.

"Need you," was what I think I mumbled, and Mack picked up speed.

"God, Frances," he groaned. "I never…never thought this would be for me…"

I couldn't respond because his words toppled me over the edge, and Mack started going with me, and together we hit a furious pace, striving for whatever this was to become…lust gone viral, feelings, or just a quick and awesome lay.

Later, cleaned up, showered, and in bed, my head lay on Mack's chest while he ran his fingers through my hair. I remembered there was one detail I hadn't shared. I didn't know why I hadn't said anything. Maybe because I wanted to know where the Jimmy and Rosie mission ended, and Mack and Frankie began.

Mack interrupted my mental war. "What's got your head working overtime? I can practically feel you overthinking."

I closed my eyes and spoke. "Remember the first set of letters?"

I felt Mack nod behind me.

"And they spoke about the lilies? And you said that was Silky's first scent?"

"Yes." His answer was raspy as his hand traveled down my arm and up again.

"I should have told you then, and I don't know why I didn't," I rambled. "Maybe to protect me, or Paps, or you, or all of us."

"What's going on?"

He didn't sound impatient or mad, which blanketed me in compassion. "I don't want there to be secrets, okay?"

"No secrets."

"My middle name is Lily. Before you say anything, it could be a coincidence, or just dumb luck…"

His fingers interlaced with mine, and I went on with my longwinded explanation.

"I wasn't sure if I should tell you after you read the letters. It's probably meaningful to note…I thought about it for a long time after I read them. Although it means my parents might know some of the story or not. Who knows? My Paps was influential and could have asked them to give me the name. Or maybe my mom really liked the name. I'm not close with them much anymore, and I never really asked them…"

"Or maybe it was about Jimmy keeping a piece of Rosie with him."

I felt a tear well in the corner of my eye. "Maybe. You're not mad?"

"No. You told me when you were ready. Solving Jimmy and Milly's love affair was never my mission. If anything, it makes me think you're even more meant for me with Lily as your middle name."

Without interruptions, the rest of the weekend passed in a flurry of easygoing times and intimacy.

It was hard not to get swept into false hopes of a budding fairy tale.

CHAPTER Nineteen

FRANKIE

"I have a surprise for you," I told Mack on Friday when he called. It was mid-September and the weeks since we'd been in the Hamptons had passed in a flurry of work and seeing one another.

First, Mack went back to Paris and London, before heading to China to check on a packaging plant. The scope of his business was enormous, and I was beginning to understand how hard he worked to get where he was today.

I did take on two new customers, finding myself motivated to work harder and smarter—like the man I was falling for.

"Oh, yeah? Are you taking up golf? That would be an amazing surprise…"

He'd missed a couple of golf gatherings due to being with me, and had taken to teasing me over my lack of playing.

"Sure, I've been secretly practicing while you were away…" I giggled.

"I'm not really a surprise kind of guy. I like to know what I'm walking into," Mack responded, knowing I'd been joking.

When I'd called Corey to double-check on Mack's availability, he'd said as much— "He's not going to love a surprise, Frankie, babe," were his exact words. "I almost got fired a few times for trying to pull one over on the guy."

"I'm willing to risk it," I'd told him. "I'm persuasive, you know?"

Now I reassured Mack.

"You will like this, I'm pretty sure. It's a simple surprise."

"Does it involve you?"

"Yes…" I couldn't help the laugh escaping me. Mack had a way of making everything feel easy and fun, as if I were young-*ish* again.

"I have to swing by the office and head out to Westchester. I want to see the remodel on the store. They've added a few new tester areas in the front since the vandalism, and I haven't seen the layout. Dinner later? And you can surprise away?"

That was what I was hoping he'd say. "Okay, how about at my place? I have to see one client for a French cuff emergency and then I can head home and cook. Might be nice to eat something decent?"

"Are you sure? I don't mind going out…"

Things I'd learned about Mack over the last month: he didn't like to make extra work for others; he'd rather spend money on getting something done than ask someone a favor; and he was allergic to leaning on anyone for support. Basically, he'd been emotionally abandoned by his mother, and convinced himself it was best not to be reliant on anyone.

There was no French cuff emergency; I was already in my kitchen with my own sleeves rolled up.

Mack and I had eaten out so many times, but I wanted to do something a bit different to mark this day. Despite going out often, Mack liked his space. He'd come to kickboxing with me two more times—requesting our own corner, reserving several extra spots to allow for the privacy. I kept wanting to settle into a more regular home-based routine, but Mack clearly tried to be a fancy-pants. Well, not this weekend, he wasn't.

"I'm sure," I told him despite being slightly worried later when I opened the door, wearing a party hat and a bright pink apron over my long sleeve T-shirt and jeans, in bare feet and minimal makeup.

With an eyebrow raised, Mack entered my place. He seemed to be looking for someone else.

"Is anyone here?" he asked, either reading my mind or being overly panicked.

"No, who would be here?"

"No one. Never mind. Have you been stalking me again?" He growled the question while half smiling.

I felt a small grin spread over my face. "Maybe a tiny bit of internet searching. Fact-finding, you know?"

Mack circled me, gathering me close, pulling me into his chest and kissing the top of my head. I heard him breathe me in before he spoke. "Hello, Frances. I missed you…until this very moment when I realized you were up to something naughty."

"I knew it!" I taunted, not moving from his arms.

"But the thing is, I don't do birthday parties…" His breath tickled the top of my head as he spoke.

Slipping out of his embrace, I stood with a hand on my hip. "This year you do, Mackenzie Miller." I watched his mouth quirk and knew something sinister was going to come out.

"I also don't do Mackenzie. I think I've mentioned this before."

"Okay, sir. No full name, and a private birthday celebration, not a party."

"Do I get to do whatever I want with you?"

"We will see if you behave."

He strode over to the window and noted, "It's starting to rain. And since we're stuck inside, I can think of some things I'd like to do…

Things I want to do very badly."

"I bet," I said while working my way back over to him. Since the night in the pool, this was our way. We teased, poked, prodded, and let our actions do the talking. "First, we'll celebrate your birthday. Which, according to the internet, is today. Lucky forty-seven…and then we'll eat cake before we do all the things you want."

"Is that so? All of them?"

I nodded.

"You don't even know what they are."

"That's the thing. When it comes to you, I don't care." Clamping my mouth shut, I couldn't believe the brazenness spilling from my lips.

Mack didn't seem to mind. He pulled me in for a brutal kiss, giving me all he had, slipping the hat off my head and running his fingers through my hair. He held the strands in the back and kept me steady while his lips crushed into mine.

When he broke free, he whispered, "Thank you. It's been a long while since I did anything more than grab a scotch and a cigar with my friends."

"No cigars here, but I have some other lucky surprises," I mentioned while walking to the open kitchen area.

"Is that so?"

Nodding, I said, "I do have mishy-mashy soup."

A veil of sadness washed over his face.

Startled, I asked, "What? I called Connie, and she told me the recipe. I thought it would be fun to replicate one of Milly's recipes for you."

Turning, Mack spoke to the window. "She used to make the soup for me. All the time. I never knew its origin or that she made it for Jimmy until I met you and read the letters. Now it feels strange, like it was their thing, not ours."

"Maybe that's the point. It was Milly's way of bridging the gap between you and Paps."

159

Facing me, he walked toward the kitchen. "Thank you, again." He spoke softly. "Not forgetting her cooking, specifically mishy-mashy soup, was one of the tasks in her letter to me. And I've neglected the delicacy for a moment. But here you are—my Feisty Frankie—not letting me forget a thing." He put his arm around me, his hand at the small of my back and whispered, "Frances, I'm so lucky to have met you. But my birthday? Really?"

Needing a breather from the serious moment, I joked, "Well, taste the soup first before you make proclamations. I didn't tell anyone, if that matters to you."

"It's been a long time since anyone cared about the day, that's all. Milly always did." He paced while speaking, presumably not wanting to ruin the occasion. "I had a girlfriend in college who was going to fix me and all my issues…and then keep me."

"You had a girlfriend? The self-proclaimed commitment-phobe? Scandalous!" I feigned shock, clutching my imaginary pearls.

"I did, but in terms of importance she's not that high up. We were young, she was disillusioned, and well, that's a story for another time. On this very day in prehistoric times, she blabbed about my birthday to the whole football team and planned a surprise party for me after a huge home game. I didn't want any part of it. The worst was she'd known I'd invited my mom to the game and witnessed her no-show performance, and still wanted me to carry on as if nothing happened."

I approached him slowly, running my hands up his chest, placing a small kiss above his heart. I wanted to repair what had been done to him more than my next breath. "I didn't invite anyone or blab about your birthday, so we're in the clear."

I was desperate to be the positive energy he needed. And yet here we stood, neither of us able to make the necessary declarations.

"It's like you ordered rain for my birthday so we could have soup… and stay in… If the weather was better, we could have gone to the Hamptons." Instead of initiating any more serious conversation, that was what he said.

"Come on, sit," I told him, taking the hint, pointing to the counter and stools.

"Drink? I think a scotch goes with soup?"

"Scotch goes with anything."

I poured Mack his cocktail and a healthy glass of red wine for myself, and we sat and chatted over our drinks. I mentioned my new client being in the restaurant biz, and Mack said, "You're lucky I'm not the jealous type. All these powerful men, calling you and working with you."

"Oh, is the birthday boy having a pity party?" I teased.

"A small one…"

"Aw, poor baby." I leaned in and kissed him as the words floated off my tongue. He tasted smoky, like expensive scotch, and I'd quickly grown to be a fan of the flavor.

"So where's the soup? I'll be the one to let you know if it's any good."

"Ha. Connie walked me through the process. It's a lot of steps," I told Mack. I went over to the stovetop where the soup was in a ginormous pot and lifted the lid, the salty aroma filling the air.

"I remember Milly making it. She took such pride in the whole situation. I always chalked it up to her love of home cooking, but there seems to be more to the recipe now."

"There certainly is." I ladled the soup into bowls, seeing all the ingredients I'd lovingly added, and couldn't help the warm feeling spreading in my chest.

Lifting my gaze, I caught Mack's hair looking perfectly messed, and a boyish grin on his face, contradicted by the small lines at the corner of his eyes. And the feeling inside me spiked.

I hadn't known how this would go when I vaguely remembered Mack's birthday. I'd checked Google and sure enough I was right, wondering why he hadn't mentioned it. Then I'd thought about how abandoned he'd felt as a child and I knew I had to do something special. A fancy dinner out didn't seem like the answer. That was when I'd decided on an ode to home cooking and Milly.

As we carried our dishes back to the bar, I prayed my hunch was right.

Before taking a bite, Mack stopped and looked at me. "This is a pretty good birthday. One Milly would have approved of. Homemade food, a drink at home with someone I care for... Wait, is there cake? Milly had a huge sweet tooth."

"You'll have to wait and see," I teased. Of course there was cake, but in the moment, I wanted to keep this man guessing—it was turning out to be fun.

Mack waggled his eyebrows at me and went to take a spoonful of his soup. I watched him ladle a bite with spinach and a dumpling into his mouth with curiosity.

"Mmmm...tastes like Milly's." He glowed like a kid on Christmas morning.

I felt myself grinning while taking a bite myself.

"Tell me what Connie said," Mack asked with his focus on me.

"She says happy birthday."

"I thought you didn't tell anyone?"

"Just Connie. She doesn't count. I'm sure she knew from Milly. Okay, and my friend, Rachel. I can't lie, but Rachel also doesn't count."

He took another spoonful, this one including a bite of meatball. "Later I want to hear about this Rachel, but first get on with Connie."

"Bossy?"

"It's my birthday, I can boss if I want to—"

I cut Mack off. This version of him was too cute and corny, and was giving me heart palpitations over my growing feelings for the man. "Connie said that she and your grandma would play around in the kitchen after school. She laughed when she told me what she referred to as their little secret—Rosie would try things she wasn't allowed to eat at home. She even ate a ham sandwich one time."

"*What?*"

"Yep, a ham sandwich. Connie told me. Anyway, she said they liked to mix and match their recipes and they came up with mishy-mashy soup together. It was basically chicken and dumplings—"

"Matzo balls," Mack interrupted. "We call them matzo balls."

"They're hard to make, I'll tell you that much. Rachel, who is Jewish, said she hates making them. Hers always come out too hard."

"I wouldn't know…never tried making them."

"Well, they are difficult. You start the soup with a whole chicken, skimming the scum—Connie's word, not mine—off the top as it boils, before adding a celery stalk, half an onion, and chopped carrots. While that's going you make meatballs…since it's a combination matzo ball and wedding soup. You also assemble the matzo ball mixture and refrigerate it for twenty minutes or so before tossing half a bouillon cube into the broth. Then you start rolling and adding the matzo balls and drop in the meatballs after it boils. Finally, it simmers for a long time, lid ajar. Oh! The spinach goes in last. You add that when you turn the heat down. Whew…that's a lot to explain."

Mack set his spoon down and kissed my cheek. "Thank you. It all sounds like a foreign language to me, but it's very good and I'm loving every bite. I can see why Jimmy fell for my grandma."

"Would have been easier if he fell for Connie," I said.

"But he didn't. The heart falls for who the heart wants. There must be some saying like that."

Much later, after we ate and were hanging out, I told Mack about Rachel and how she'd become like a sister. We talked some more about my parents and their siding with Jeremy, and of course I asked Mack what he used to do on his birthdays.

"I can tell you, but then I might have to kill you…"

"I can keep a secret."

"I'm not so sure about that," he teased before going somber. His voice soft, still deep, he spoke. "It's not my favorite day. My mom left on my birthday. That was the actual day she chose. Left me a card and a present, said she'd be back soon, and never returned. Milly tried to make up for it with birthday pool parties and sleepovers. Nothing really worked. Then there was the college catastrophe. Needless to say, that was when I banned girlfriends."

My hand wove its way into his fingers and my thumb caressed his. "I'm sorry. I didn't know." I mentally scolded myself for asking.

"About my one serious relationship? It's so far in the rearview. And as for my mom, how could you know? I try to keep any discussion of her out of the spotlight. She knows where I am and how successful I've been, and I'm not looking to invite her in to any more details. I don't want her in my life now. She never was a part of it when I needed her, so opening up the subject would be bad for all those involved."

"Well, I hope today was okay. I wanted to incorporate some piece of Milly."

"It's my new favorite way to celebrate."

Mine too, I thought but worried if this type of happiness was sustainable…

In the past, it hadn't been.

CHAPTER Twenty

MACK

My phone rang as I was lacing up my shoes on Sunday. I hesitated to answer since I'd come to the golf club to escape the world, but I knew it would blow back on me.

Scolding myself for not being the one to call months ago, I answered on the third ring.

"You're a few days late," was my brash greeting, knowing the other party could take the harassment.

I knew why he was calling; he was the only one who ever called this time of year. Not Susie or her husband, or their spawn. They only called when they needed something.

"I know. Jet lag is a real bitch. Cassandra and I were in Rome for two weeks. A third honeymoon kind of thing, living the good life."

"Must be nice. Retirement, I mean. But you've been married for at least two decades, I think," I told my longtime friend Teddy.

"You ever heard of the saying, 'happy wife, happy life'? I live by it, bro. As for Rome—fuck, man, you could go for a year and it wouldn't hurt your bottom line, Miller."

I smiled to no one, sitting up and leaning against the locker. The golf club had a no-phones policy in the area, but no one was going to say a word to me.

Miller—not Mack or Millsy or Mackenzie—was what all my football teammates called me way back in undergraduate against the rolling hills of Virginia. I was the soccer player turned kicker, and they were the unlikely crew who accepted me. Most of us had lost touch other than holiday wishes and cards or occasional favors, but not Theodore and me.

"If I went a year without working, what would I do? Lose my mind?"

"I have some ideas." I could almost see the ass smirking.

I closed my eyes and could feel my crow's feet crinkling up from my grin. This guy had been one of the few people who'd broken through my hard exterior. Maybe one of three or four people aside from my grandmother...and the last person only happened recently.

"I don't want to know about those ideas. Tell your wife," I joked with him, laughing out loud to an empty room.

He finally cut to the chase for the call. "Happy birthday, man."

He didn't know there was someone in my world, and part of me didn't want to let him in on it. Frances had taken up sacred space in my heart. So much so, it hurt thinking it might not last.

Teddy's call also happened to be the one part of my birthday I didn't share with her... In fact, I hadn't spoken about Teddy to Frances at all. I didn't know if it was his unspoken allegiance with Milly's ghost or what. The pair haunted me regularly, and admitting all that to someone who'd captured my heart felt hard and heavy.

We'd already delved into the letters and the family history tying us together, and while she hadn't seen Milly's letter to me...I guess in the end, I didn't want to disappoint Frances too.

If she knew how much I'd let my friend and my grandmother

down, surely she'd think less of me.

Teddy knew I hated my birthday with a vengeance, yet he called me every single year. He would certainly get the significance of actually sharing the day with someone.

"How's Arizona?"

"Changing the subject already? Tell me you didn't sit in like a lonely piece of shit this year, sipping on Lagavulin?"

I'd have to tell him eventually, and better now than when it fell apart, right? "You're not going to believe this, but I didn't sit in. Well, I stayed in with a certain someone. Celebrated the occasion this year with a home-cooked meal, a half-decent scotch, and a beautiful woman."

"No way. You're shitting me. Here I was, feeling sorry for your ass, and you keep this from me."

Sitting back up, I ran a hand through my hair and blew out a long breath. "I didn't plan to commemorate the day. But this woman, the one I've been seeing, used Google to trick me. Planned a dinner…got a recipe, and all this crap I didn't deserve."

"Whoa, a woman you're seeing and I didn't know? Google? What? She didn't know your birthday and surprised you? I remember a time that a b-day surprise went very poorly. Back up and start from the beginning…you know I'm your shrink."

Teddy was somewhat right; he'd stepped in when I needed him most and wouldn't admit I needed help. I could've told Teddy I was on my way to play eighteen holes, but he wouldn't have cared, so I filled him in on Frances.

"What you're telling me is this blond terror has seeped so far into your heart that she surprised you with a birthday celebration, cooking for you from some secret family recipe, all the while doing a deep dive into your family history, including your mom and some guy your grandmother was in love with?"

"That's about it."

Teddy banged some surface with his hand and yelled, "God damn,

I knew it would happen. Last time a woman surprised you with your birthday, you went AWOL. Frances—winner, winner, chicken dinner. I gotta get out there and meet this woman. Good thing I retired."

"I'll keep you posted. Don't get ahead of yourself." I issued the warning, but I knew Teddy wouldn't obey. After playing in the League, he'd coached football in Arizona before retiring and day-trading and investing in real estate. He'd done well for himself, and I'd always watched his success with pride.

"See you soon, birthday boy. I have to go tell Cassandra all this. She will not believe Mackenzie Miller is shacking up. Tell her we are heading to New York," Teddy said boisterously, knocking me from an emotional moment.

"Ted—"

Of course he disconnected the call before I could argue.

"Like this?"

Later, Frances wiggled her ass against me while I helped her hold a seven iron.

I'd played eighteen on my lonesome. It was by design. I wasn't up for the company or the competition; I needed time to think.

That was until Frances texted and all thoughts of being by myself flew south. I wanted to see her, so what did I do? I sent a car to get her and bring her out to Westchester to hit golf balls.

"Actually, more like this," I said while helping Frances correct her posture. Repositioning her hands on the club, I shadowed her movements as she swung.

She might need some professional lessons, I thought, but I forced myself to not mention that her ball didn't go very far.

"How about a drink?" Frances finally suggested, frustrated with her performance.

"Let's go," was all I said. "How was your day?" I asked her over my mule and her glass of cabernet.

"Sunday, so no work, as you know. And!" Her whole face lit up as she said the one-syllable word.

"And?" I inquired, needing to know what had the beautiful creature so excited.

"I made another recipe. Connie also talked me through a dessert she learned to make with Milly!"

Taking a slug of my mule, I waited to hear about the dessert, thinking I'd probably eaten it a million times and never known the significance.

"I'm not sure I did it any justice, but Connie said your grandma made a mean apple cake. Those were her words. She said she taught Milly how to make fruitcake. Can you imagine? And Milly taught her this apple cake." I couldn't resist my hand slipping over Frances's fingers. "Fruitcake. Isn't that crazy? Did she ever make it?"

My head shook. "No, I can't say she ever made a fruitcake, but she did make apple cake. Twice a year. Always for the Jewish holidays and usually once more, around Thanksgiving."

"It's good. It may not be as dense as it should be, but I can give you a piece when you drop me off."

"You perfected the soup, so I'm sure the cake is perfect."

"You know what? I need to spend a few days with Connie and catalog all these recipes. Write them down, put them in a Word document, save them!"

The need to be closer to Frances overtook me and I leaned in and kissed her cheek, breathing in her scent. Today it was lilies mixed with excitement. I wanted it all for myself.

"Would that be okay? Me, making a keepsake of Milly's recipes?"

"Of course. She was one of the better parts of my life. I'm not going to lie—I wish I'd known about your Paps and that part of her life. But for whatever reason, I didn't."

Frances took a sip of her wine and brought her hand to my cheek.

"She was good to you, and I'm glad you had that. Your mom missed out on so much, and I'm not going to be like this mystery girl from your past trying to fix that—"

"That's all she was…a girl," I interrupted. "We were young, and I didn't know anything about life, love, feelings, or shit. In fact, I spoke to an old friend today…"

Frances leaned back, eyeing me. "Her?"

"No, her name was Brittany and I have no idea where she is or what she's done since the night we broke up during our junior year. It was an ugly breakup, but it's irrelevant. What I didn't tell you about my birthday was that my friend, Teddy, from college, calls every year."

"He does? You said cigars and whiskey with friends… Is he one of them?" Thankfully, Frances was back in my personal space, her hand woven through mine, our drinks discarded.

"No. Teddy was my teammate in college. Big, daunting guy, who taught me about feelings. He caught on to my mommy issues right away and confronted me. Told me to deal with my emotions while he stood towering over me in the weight room. Turns out his mom slipped out in the middle of the night too, leaving him and his sister. In all the years since then, I haven't talked much about my mom with anyone but him."

This time, it was Frances who brought her lips to my cheek before she whispered, "I'm glad you had that, and now you have me."

I didn't ask—*could I keep her?*

CHAPTER
Twenty-One

MACK

"What are you doing for Thanksgiving?" Frances cocked her head and nervously twisted a strand of hair while asking me.

My hand jutted out and stilled her fingers—I hated seeing her unnerved. Over the last two months, I'd noticed it wasn't often. But when it occurred, it did something to me. Occasionally, she appeared to have to work up a lot of nerve. "Does that mean you are free?"

It was the Monday before the holiday. We were sitting at my breakfast bar, each drinking a coffee, and I was returning a few emails.

She rolled her eyes. "Don't answer a question with a question, Mr. Miller. Do I need to ask Corey?"

"Please don't. He'll try to get me to go to some big formal turkey dinner at a boutique hotel, the one he's been talking about nonstop. No, thank you."

I knew Frances had been struggling with the holiday; her parents had invited her, but she hadn't said yes or no. Yesterday, she came over after I got home from a mall scouting trip in Minnesota, and we'd ordered sushi takeout and watched a movie. It had been easy, but clearly we hadn't discussed much.

"I am free," Frances said to me, "but no obligation. I was wondering…"

"You know I'm free and I want to be with you, which is quickly becoming my favorite thing to do." I gathered her close and kissed her cheek.

"Other than work," Frances teased.

"I have to pay bills."

"Yes, I can see you're struggling."

I loved how Frances took in stride my need to be the best, to do better than generations before me, and be as successful as possible. I leaned in and kissed her cheek again, inhaling her, our latest scent lingering on her neck. Another tidbit I adored—Frances had started using all Silky's products.

I moved on with the conversation, tabling my feelings. "Does this mean you told your parents no?" Sitting back and picking up my mug, I gave her time to answer.

"I did. Thanks to not working and you being away and, oh—I forgot to say Rachel is dating some new guy. Anyway, I had all weekend to think about it, and I decided it was a very firm no. I called them and explained my feelings. They denied picking sides with Jeremy but were going to die on the hill that I should be more than thrilled with my settlement. I think they're mad I didn't give them anything financially…I don't know. It doesn't matter. I'm not going, and I'm available."

"Good. Can I let my house manager order a dinner for us here? I'd love to go to the Hamptons, but I need to be near the office with Black Friday. Though I don't have to go in unless needed…"

That was another change over the last two months. I had much more arranged, and fewer people around doing tasks, like making coffee.

Frances and I deserved privacy, so the cleaning and housekeeping staff came in during the day and set up the kitchen for the following morning.

"That's fine with me. I like our little holidays."

"I do too," I said, standing and pulling Frances into my arms, kissing the top of her head.

We'd celebrated the Jewish New Year that way—a small private dinner for two, and remembering Milly. Of course Frances made the apple cake, and it was more than perfect. The exact right density, and this prompted her to solidify her plans to put together a cookbook with Connie.

With emotions swirling, I'd shown Frances my letter that evening, and she'd cried when I'd mentioned she was helping me do what Milly dreamed of for me. It was the first year in a while that I hadn't gone to the cemetery, following another one of Milly's requests.

Now, as I held Frances in her robe, I couldn't help my hand slipping inside and cupping the side of her breast. Goose bumps broke out on her skin as I rounded her nipple. As I pinched the tiny bundle of nerves, I watched Frances's head fall back and I kissed my way up her neck.

"I have to go to work," Frances mumbled.

"You do?"

"Yes, I have a before-the-office appointment with one of my customers."

"I'd like a before-the-office appointment," I joked, but I really only wanted to see Frances every day…

"You're seeing me right now," Frances whispered into my chest, nuzzling closer.

"It's never enough."

There were a lot of bold statements like this between us, but no declarations of love or where this was going. Maybe that was on me. I didn't know.

"Later? I'm going to run with Rachel. She wants to give me the 411.

After, dinner? Maybe I'll cook?"

I couldn't help the laugh escaping me as Frances rambled.

"What?" she asked, pretending to glare at me. It was all show. Tough, kickboxing Frances couldn't hurt anyone if she tried—except for the time she hit me.

"I love when you talk dirty, like cooking for me…and I'm glad you have that…with Rachel." I truly was, knowing Frances didn't have many people. I didn't say as much because I wouldn't dare hurt her feelings.

I'd loved meeting Rachel for drinks in October. We'd gone to a pumpkin espresso martini tasting that was horrible and ended back here at my place for a better round of drinks. Rachel had teased me, asking if I had Manischewitz, and we all laughed. Yet I hadn't suggested we meet my buddies yet, but I guessed it would happen eventually. Maybe I needed to push the agenda…

That was where my thoughts were as Frances scooted away, and I realized what a fixture she'd become at my apartment and how much I liked it. She started to head toward the back bedroom to get ready, and while I could tell she was in work mode, I thought about when I should tell her that I love her.

"She's silly in love. I mean, gaga for this guy in a way she never was for her husband," Frances told me much later that night.

We were in her bed, after she'd cooked us this amazing pasta alla Norma. She was lying on her side, running figure eights on my bare chest.

"Did you like her husband?" I asked, not sure whether exes were a good topic. Frances knew I didn't have anyone serious to speak of due to my own restrictions, but we hadn't spoken about her ex since that night during the summer.

"He was fine. Just fine, you know? Not anything great or bad…"

I felt myself nodding. "Why did she marry him, then?"

"I think because everyone was doing it. She felt pressure. It was okay because they just went their separate ways when it was over, split their money, and moved on."

"No kids, right?" Immediately, I wanted to punch myself for asking.

"No," Frances answered and looked up at me, running a hand down my cheek. "It's okay to talk about kids around me. I'm not permanently broken or scarred, other than my honey pot still left over..."

She glanced down at her belly, which I'd caught her doing upon occasion, and this was an area I was ill equipped to handle. I didn't sense she was fishing for compliments like most women when they said they were "fat."

"Hey, your body was trying to do something miraculous. It just didn't work out that time..."

Damn, watching Frances's face, I knew I messed up.

"Any time. I'm thirty-eight, and I don't think these things get easier with age. So that was my time."

"I'm sorry...I'm not saying the right thing." My palm ran over the area on her lower abdomen she called her honey pot. "I like every inch of you. And this, which isn't there, is beautiful. You're *beautiful*, inside and out, and every part of your story that brought you to me..."

She rested her forehead on my shoulder and spoke softly. "I don't know where this is going, and I promise you I'm not looking for you to say anything, but I want you to know that I may not be able to have kids. Not maybe, but likely definitely."

She kissed me, and I kissed her back, trying to convey how I felt with my actions since I couldn't seem to sort out the words.

It was some kind of cruel joke that at forty-seven I still couldn't come up with the right way to tell someone I loved them.

CHAPTER
Twenty-Two

FRANKIE

*D*espite not knowing what we were doing with one another, what either of our intentions were, or where this was going, Thanksgiving was one of the best. Simply perfect.

Mack had a million-course dinner delivered and we used some fancy china dishes I wasn't even sure why he owned. And we finished a bottle of wine in front of the fire, sitting on a blanket, our backs to the sofa, legs in front of us, thighs touching.

"Actually, you should thank Corey," Mack joked, smoothing his palm down my thigh, goose bumps lighting up my leg. "He ordered the food."

Running my hand down his arm, I inquired, "More important, tell me—why do you have more kitchen and dining stuff than a bridezilla?"

Mack turned to face me, smirking, and asked, "Jealous?"

I squeezed his arm. "No…no, I am not…"

"I feel wounded. You really know how to make a guy feel like he's on top of the world…" We teased back and forth for a bit until Mack admitted, "My designer. I had nothing to do with any of it. I bought the place on spec. I used to live in a pre-war place down in the Village, and when I relocated my offices up here, I decided to move myself. Bought this based on the floor plan and let her do her thing."

Sipping my wine, I listened.

"I mean, Sherry, interior designer to only the most selective clientele, said I needed 'all the trimmings.' Corey gave her my American Express card, and she had at it. I think this was the first time I used those fancy plates."

I couldn't help my hand reaching out and running down his cheek. "I'm honored to have been the one to use the fancy plates, as you call them."

He took my wineglass and set it behind him on the side table, disposing of his right next to it before cupping my face. "Paper plates, expensive shit, it doesn't matter. I'm honored to have spent this day with you, Frances. *Beautiful Frances*, it's the first holiday in a long while I've spent with someone who mattered."

I mattered.

It was the kindest thing anyone had ever told me—after feeling discarded by everyone in my life.

Mack ran his lips along my chin. "I can feel your brain working overtime—don't. Enjoy the moment. It's Thanksgiving and I'm thankful for you."

Our lips met. At first, the kiss was soft and tender, two people showing feelings rather than telling. Our mouths picked up fervor as we slid toward the floor, my back resting on the soft rug, Mack hovering over me. His hand slipped under my silk blouse, his thumb and pointer finger finding my nipple. A low moan escaped my chest as he twisted and plucked the tender spot, my legs squirming under him, seeking friction.

"Mack," I whispered.

"I got you," he said, his hand traversing south, leaving my nipple cold and lonely until he found my heat.

As my body temperature soared, Mack took me there with a hand shoved between my velour leggings and my core. It wasn't a scene out of a movie where the couple is naked and the flames are flickering off their smooth skin as they make love in front of the fire. It was raw and wicked and decadent. I pitched myself up a tiny bit to yank Mack's shirt over his head. Thankfully, he'd gone with a Henley rather than a button-down. My lips sucked harder on his nipple as I began to reach a crescendo, thanks to Mack's fingers.

"I want you," he drawled while sucking on my earlobe, his thumb pressing down on the exact right spot, stars clouding my eyes.

"I'm there." I half whispered, the other part shrieked. He didn't let up as my climax hit, rather wrung it out of me before shoving my pants down, fast as hell, my small thong going with them. I'd been barefoot for hours so there were no shoes in the way.

I tried to help with Mack's pants, but he wouldn't have it. "In a hurry," he grumbled, standing and shucking them down.

I couldn't help the smile that broke out on my face. *Mackenzie Miller is in a hurry for me…*

And he was. Without pause, Mack was back down on the floor, ghosting over me, his hot breath on my neck. I felt butterflies swimming in my gut and a pulsing tingle in between my legs.

"Please," I spoke, my voice raspy with want and need. He entered me slowly, decadently, taking his time with each draw until the veins bulged in his neck. Running my hand over his stubble, I mumbled, "Faster."

I wanted it and knew he needed it. He didn't wait to oblige.

Picking up speed, Mack slid in and out at a brutal pace and it wasn't long before the stars hit me again and he was shaking inside me. We waited out each sensation, Mack pulsing, me drawing every last wave from him—happily.

Afterward, we lay there for a while, neither of us speaking, only touching, quietly savoring the moment. Our breaths started to even, and our damp skin began to cool and dry. It was the most fulfilled I'd felt in a long time, or forever. Sated from sex, not starving for affection, and complete in a way I hadn't known existed for me…

The following morning I woke up tangled in Mack's sheets. Turning, I caught the man who'd left me feeling all kinds of ways before falling asleep, his features still and content. While watching his chest rise and fall peacefully, I felt something deep in my chest. I wondered how anyone could have hurt him so much…

"Morning," he grumbled with his eyes closed. "I feel you watching me, and I like it." His voice was still sleepy.

"It's becoming a bad habit of mine. Staying over, never knowing if I have a clean pair of panties and not caring. And of course, surveying you while you sleep." Squeezing my eyes shut, I growled. "Ugh, I didn't mean that to come out like that, asking for more. Everything is perfect as is. I'm not probing."

Sitting up, he pulled me into his arms. "Shhh," he whispered into my forehead, his breath tickling my hairline. "*More* is what I was thinking too."

I was about to ask what kind of more when Mack's phone buzzed, interrupting the moment. I wasn't sure if it was a blessing or a curse.

"One sec," he said. "It's Corey. And I want to continue the *more* talk, but I have to hear what he needs."

I took advantage of him answering the call and went to the bathroom before padding toward the kitchen. Someone had come in during the wee hours and set up coffee service and laid out a fruit platter, and I wondered what Mack's childhood was like when it came to holiday mornings. Did his dad spend time with him? Certainly, Milly was a cornerstone. I smiled to no one. At least he'd had my Paps's Rosie…

Pouring a cup of coffee, I heard Mack strolling in while on the phone.

"Yes. That's fine. Sydney can handle all this, and tell the tech department to attach the discount to every cart. We don't want any unnecessary complaints," he said, before he disconnected the call.

I walked toward the panoramic window in the corner of the living space and took in the blue sky, betting it was brisk and cold despite the sunny day.

"Gorgeous," Mack whispered, his arm snaking around my middle.

"It is."

"I meant you. In my place. I'd like more, you know?"

Turning, I asked, "Everything okay? With work?" It was a feeble attempt at distracting Mack.

"Yes. There was a tech error with the website, and it's being resolved. Hopefully, all smooth sailing from here…but none of it matters. Don't try and derail me…"

"What? Me?" I feigned innocence, but he wasn't buying it.

Mack continued to gaze into my eyes. "When you're ready, we'll talk about it. But know this—I'll only wait so long for you to say you're ready to chat."

I ran my hand over his bare chest, hoping he'd say we should go back to bed—the ultimate distraction.

"I think this corner would be a perfect place for a tree and, ironically, tonight is the start of Hanukkah. It's one of those years where the Jewish holidays are early," was what I got instead.

I nodded, knowing the Jewish calendar didn't always sync up with ours. "I don't know how it works, but your holidays fall on different days every year."

"Something along the lines of the Jewish calendar following the moon."

We stood like that, my hand on his chest, his lips meeting the top of my head, chatting by the window. It was commonplace and special in equal measure.

"What do you think about a tree in this space? Is it a good place?"

he asked.

"Are you rhyming on purpose?" I couldn't help but tease. I had no idea where this conversation was heading.

"No, I am most certainly not rhyming on purpose. I am waiting to hear your opinion."

My head tipped back and I peeked to the side to look at the spot he was mentioning. "What I want to know is what does a tree have to do with the first night of Hanukkah?"

Mack let out a laugh and his breath ghosted my cheek. "Well, we were about to talk about more, and you're making me wait," he said while taking my hand in his, "so I decided how about we start by making room for both of our traditions. Then we can talk about making a place here for you…in a steadier fashion. I know you love your apartment and it's all yours and I don't want to diminish that."

"I don't want to wash away your traditions or replace them. I don't want to disrespect what you believe in or Milly, or what she stood for…" I interrupted.

"Shhh," he said, bringing an index finger to my lips. "We are not diminishing anything. Milly believed in love conquers all, and I know you would never strip me of my past, and I wouldn't do that to you."

He waited for a response, weaving our hands together, but I was in a trance, stuck on his *love conquers all* statement.

Mack took it upon himself to bring me back to the moment. "A tree it is! First comes the merging of customs and traditions we grew up with—"

"Then comes marriage…" I interrupted, foolishly.

"And a baby in a carriage."

He spoke the words, but it was my fault. I'd led with the old grade-school taunt, and he'd finished it. Yet as soon as he said it I felt the blow.

Judging by the furrow in Mack's brow, he was struck with it too. "I'm sorry, I didn't mean it like that."

Moving away, turning my back toward him and sucking in my

emotions, I took a long breath.

All this *more* talk, teasing and taunting, joking…and I was making a fool of myself. "Of course you didn't. Just like I didn't mean 'then comes marriage.' We were both caught up in the moment. Let's leave it be."

Giving us both an out, I felt relief as I made my way back to the man who had stolen my heart without trying. Kissing his pec, allowing my lips to linger, I thought about all that just flew out of our mouths.

"I know that's a lot to unpack, so why don't we start with a tree and a menorah. Some simple fun," Mack suggested, reading my mind.

I felt my head nodding against his warm skin. "Perfect," I said and meant it. I was happy for the reprieve.

In my mind, there was a lot rumbling around and too many questions. But the idea of a tree and a menorah was kind of interesting… I hadn't thought about what Christmas signified to me since losing Jeremy and the baby, other than a busy and fruitful time at work. I also never considered leaving my apartment or what that would say about me.

"It's a nice place. Mine, I mean," I blurted out a few minutes later, after we had retreated to refill our coffee mugs.

"It is," Mack agreed.

I stated the obvious. "This is nicer."

"It's bigger, that's all. Look, we can table this talk for another time. I was thinking aloud and prematurely."

A grin spread across his face, hitting the corner of his eyes, and it was another reason why I was falling for Mackenzie Miller. He knew how to read a room and gave me an easy escape.

"So, a tree? Real or fake?" The man in my mind changed the subject again.

"Are you sure? I mean, Christmas was mostly magical when I was a kid, but now it's a hectic time at work for both of us and not much more than a beautiful escape in the city."

"I'm sure. I haven't lit the menorah with someone else, other than my aunt Susie, in a long while. Now tell me, what do you usually get? Real or fake?"

Running a hand through my hair, I took a beat to gather my emotions. This was all coming so fast—

Blowing out a breath, I answered softly. "I usually get one of those little real ones, for the corner…of my place."

"Real one it is. But big and bold."

"*B*aruch atah…"

"Baruh atah." I repeated the prayer with Mack.

"*Chhhh*, like a rumble in the back of your throat." He desperately tried to help me make the correct sound.

"You sound like you're gargling mouthwash," I couldn't help but blurt out.

"I see you're getting it," he joked right back before kissing my cheek.

As we continued to say the prayer, Mack lit the first candle in the menorah. He had it set on a glass tray facing the window as soft jazz spilled out of his speakers.

"Thank you," I told Mack, taking his hand. "That was beautiful."

"No, thank you for doing that with me, and for picking the biggest, baddest tree in New York."

"Of course I chose a biggie…you told me to."

The tree place had delivered the giant fir within hours, which I knew cost a premium. Mack had offered to have it professionally decorated, but I'd insisted on stopping at my place and grabbing a few boxes of ornaments I had stashed under the bed. Together, we'd placed the mementos on the tree, and then I got it in my mind we needed the big, multicolored lights.

"Give me a second," Mack had said. In a few minutes he was back, letting me know a late lunch was on its way along with lights.

"Corey?" I'd asked.

"He was looking for a reason to see me celebrate."

The pair had discussed a few business items while we all ate Thai takeout, and then after a few jokes and laughs, Corey was gone.

"Come," Mack said now, grabbing our glasses of red wine.

We walked toward the tree and stood looking at the view.

"To more," Mack proposed.

"To more," I agreed, not knowing what more looked like and not ready to discuss it.

Taking the stem of my glass and his, Mack set them down and snatched me for an embrace. Cupping my cheeks with his palms, he kissed me. With the fireplace roaring and our lips fused we slid to the floor. Not a man in his forties and a woman in her late thirties, but young lovers, getting to know one another's bodies and hot spots.

I realized we were on the rug again, my back warm from the fire as Mack slowly pulled my blouse over my head, a button popping and rolling onto the floor. I felt the warmth of Mack's palm graze up my side as he held me close and continued to kiss me senseless. My hand flitted under his Henley and traversed his skin.

We stayed like that for a while until I couldn't take it and ripped off Mack's shirt, bringing my mouth to his nipple and sucking. A moan barreled up his throat as his head tipped back, and I continued my course, flipping him over and making my way down the rest of his body. I made quick work of his belt and pants, shrugging them down with his boxer briefs. All olive skin and muscles, from the V to his length on display, and I couldn't wait to get my mouth on him. His hips rose, beckoning me, and I slid my tongue down his hardness. All it took was one more moan and I began to work him harder, using my mouth and hand. It was like nothing I'd ever experienced in my life. With the flames flickering and the tree twinkling and Mack's groaning, it was beautiful and sensual in equal parts.

I felt Mack's hand come to the top of my head. "Frances, I want to be inside you."

He urged me to slide up his body and made quite the show out of flipping me back over and running his tongue over my bra, the heat seeping through the lace and my nipple immediately hardening.

Before I could say *I want you*, Mack was grazing my core, the stubble of his five o'clock shadow tickling my thighs. It didn't take long before I was coming apart with his mouth on me and I couldn't even find a moment to be embarrassed by how I was rubbing myself all over his face, splintering into a million pieces.

"Mack, please," I whimpered, and he didn't make me wait, quickly slithering up my body and gently pushing into me.

Our mouths fused, our tastes mingling and bodies melding as one, and I was pretty sure if this was the *more*, I wanted it all.

"I think we've spent more time on the floor than anywhere else in the last twenty-four hours," I joked, my mouth brushing against his hard chest.

"We can do something about that," Mack said, taking my hand and pulling me up with him, leading me toward the bedroom.

CHAPTER Twenty-Three

FRANKIE

A few weeks later, I jumped into a rideshare with Mack's suit and my dress, sharing a garment bag in a way I'd dreamt about but never thought was a reality. We still hadn't made any progress on any permanent moving decisions, but we were spending an adequate amount of time between one another's places. Mostly his.

Flurries fell against the darkening sky, and I smiled to myself. My life felt a tiny bit magical, and I was allowing myself to live in it. My therapist had told me a week ago that I was permitted to enjoy love and life, whatever life meant to me. When I thought about it, I hadn't enjoyed much other than work since I lost the baby.

Bringing myself back to the present, with December twenty-fifth only a few days away, it was looking as if it might be a white Christmas. I remembered being a little girl and wishing for snow every year. Paps would tell me to write to the North Pole and ask for a winter wonderland. I fell for it until I was about ten years old, and then I started to watch the weather report.

It was amazing to me how much of an optimist Paps continued to be after being shunned by Rosie's family. Made me love him a little more. I believed he never blamed Milly for the actions of her parents. She was a young girl in a time when you didn't speak up to your parents. This made me miss him a little more…and made me proud of myself for telling my parents how I felt. When I'd said no to Thanksgiving dinner and I finally let them know they'd never supported me when Jeremy left, it felt incredible. Milly never got to experience that kind of independence. Throwing open the car door, I stepped out into the dampening night.

I was thinking of the strong woman I'd never have a chance to meet when I was greeted by Mack's doorman, wearing a Santa hat and smiling at me. He held the elevator for me, saying Mack was expecting me and wishing us a *Merry Everything*. I didn't know if the last part was because Mack was Jewish, or he was being politically correct to everyone. Either way, I liked it. It had been gracious of Mack to decorate for both holidays inside his apartment, welcoming me into his life, but I had no idea in what capacity.

"Well, hello there," the man in question said as I exited the elevator.

I couldn't help the way my heart sped up and a shiver ran down my spine. The possibility of a happy ending was my kryptonite, and while I questioned what this was, I'd rather ride the high.

"Hi," I said, breathless, and Mack grabbed the garment bag, pulling me in for a kiss.

"Come on, let's see if we can have some fun before the party…"

"Grrr," I growled. "I have to get ready, and I don't want to be late… meeting your friends for the first time."

Mack nodded and snatched me in for a quick kiss, this one with tongue, and I almost rethought my stand on being tardy.

Taking the bag and unzipping it, Mack whistled at my red sequined dress…

"You haven't seen it on yet," I declared with a wink. There was something about Mack that allowed me to joke freely.

"I was whistling at the service. I don't know why I didn't switch my business sooner. I like having you hand-deliver my clothes."

"Ha ha…"

I strode through the living area, stealing my dress on the hanger from the bag, and kicking my shoes off at the edge of the carpet. I made a pit stop in front of the tree, breathing in the fresh smell before making my way to the back of the apartment to freshen up.

"Can I at least watch?" Mack trolled behind me, barefoot and wearing joggers and a T-shirt.

"Get ready, Mackenzie."

"Oh, when she pulls out my full name, I better listen."

It hit a soft spot in my heart when Mack didn't protest my using his full name like Rosie had called him. When it came to this man, more wishes built in my mind as we got dressed.

All cleaned up, Mack took our selfie in front of the fridge. I pretended to be upset over the backdrop, but it was perfect.

"How would a nice Jewish guy know where to take Christmas photos?" he said. "Also, I may or may not have a few pints of peppermint bark ice cream inside there…"

"Oh, can we forget the party and stay home?"

I turned and flung open the freezer door and sure enough there were several containers of my personal vice.

"Later, we will indulge," Mack teased with a wink.

"Hmmmm…"

He ignored the innuendo and took my hand. "Come on, let's get a Christmas photo."

Mack instructed me to stand in front of the tree and quickly took a solo picture before we went to meet Alex in the car.

"What about you?" I asked.

"I'd ruin all that beauty…" He squeezed my hand and I let the moment be.

Mack had decided to join his friends at a private party at his club. Despite being labeled a *Holiday Soiree*, it was really a Christmas party, and in the past, Mack never felt very festive—his words. But this year he did.

"What about Teddy? When do I get to meet the only person to ever get through to you?" I asked in the car, leaning my head on Mack's shoulder.

"I predict he'll soon blow into town, his gorgeous wife in tow, and wine and dine you. Tonight will be more than enough with these guys."

As we pulled in front of the refurbished warehouse on the gray-bricked road, a valet opened my door and we were ushered through an unmarked brown door. Inside, the whole place glittered and sparkled with silver and gold tinsel hanging from the ceiling, and garland dusted in glitter lining every surface.

"Welcome," the hostess said and directed us to a lounge upstairs for cocktails.

Inside the elevator, Mack tucked me in his shoulder and kissed the side of my temple. "You're stunning, beautiful in and out," he whispered, taking my hand.

Tingles fizzled in my veins at the prospect of what could be—my common theme lately. I appreciated the moment even more when we exited and were in a crush of people.

"Mack!" a tall man with a blondish beard hollered.

Mack led me in that direction where I met Spencer, who apparently was clean-shaven a few weeks ago. The two guys hugged, smacking one another on the back.

"Dude, you've been busy, and I grew a little facial hair because I'm going skiing next week…need to stay warm and other things…" Spencer explained as he joked with his arm around Mack.

"Oh? Is that so?" Mack asked, an eyebrow raised.

"Introduce me to your lady friend," Spencer said, turning to look at me.

"Frankie, this is Spencer…the guy who dragged me out on a date when I'd already fallen for you."

If I wasn't standing in a public place, I might have started to tear up. I needed to protect my heart better but these tiny truth bombs from Mack were a punch in the gut and a knife straight down the vessel pumping blood into my body.

Instead of crying happy tears, I pretended to glare at Mack before saying, "Nice to meet you, Spencer. I won't hold the date against you."

Spencer took my hand and kissed it. "Frankie, I understand Frances is only for our dear Millsy to call you."

I giggled like a schoolgirl. "Millsy has so many rules," I teased.

Spencer shined a half smile, half smirk on me. With a wink he said, "That man does have too many rules, if you ask me."

"Millsy is standing right here, so how about we get a drink and quit all the secret reveals?" Mack spoke in the third person, with an eyebrow raised.

He was absolutely adorable in an approaching-fifty way. I wanted to kiss my man's face off, but I resisted.

After Mack suggested the drink, I said, "That would be too easy."

"Easy is good…" He winked again, and I was officially smitten.

Spencer, who was watching the two of us, his gaze ping-ponging between our jabs, put his arm around me and said, "Come on, we can talk on the way. I like this little peanut."

I went easily with Mack's friend, who told me his *best bud* was a goner when it came to me. In turn, I told myself he was being kind.

Music played in the background, Bob Seger crooning "The Little Drummer Boy," and candles burned on every windowsill as we joined a few more of Mack's crew at the bar. A guy named Ryan handled introductions, and laughs were had… They'd apparently missed seeing Mack at Chelsea Piers or their exclusive golf club to hit some balls around, but he'd been busy with me, so they'd accept it.

I marveled at how the glitter theme had been carried up from downstairs. Between the holiday decorations, the champagne I'd ordered, and Mack's friends all sharing the same thoughts—*Mack was a goner*—I was certainly consumed too.

Ryan was back to detailing how Mack's golf game was going to shit because his mind had been on me. He was teasing and we were all smiling, and Mack winked at me.

Leaning in close, he whispered, "Let's not tell them I've been playing with you."

I couldn't help but giggle; I was not a decent golf partner by any stretch of the imagination. It was one of the happiest moments of my life.

"Except, one great thing is he is using the Hamptons house again! We can't wait for an invite," Ryan quickly added.

"You have your own house," Mack deadpanned, looking handsome in the charcoal gray suit we'd picked together, a Burberry tie that complemented the red in my dress, and velour loafers.

"You have a pool," Ryan clapped back to Mack.

My mind wandered to the Hamptons, the special times we'd had there, and how it had somewhat become our place. I was deep in a memory of the pool when someone tapped on my shoulder. Before turning, I noticed a sour expression color Mack's face.

"Jeremy." His name slipped out of my mouth without warning as I turned and caught sight of who was behind me.

"Frankie, you're here," he said, his tone neither warm nor inviting.

I noted the tall brunette hanging on his side, too skinny, wearing a dress a size too small, and oblivious to who I was.

"Merry Christmas," was all I could manage to say. I felt a seismic shift in the energy around me.

One second, I'd been standing with Ryan, sharing jokes, and in my mind reliving skinny-dipping with Mack. And the next, Mack was standing beside me, extending a hand to my ex-husband.

"Mackenzie Miller," he offered, not giving his nickname. This wasn't a pleasant introduction.

"Jeremy Ross."

I watched the unlikely pair shake hands, swallowing back pride, fear, and agitation.

"What are you doing here?" The question flew out of my mouth faster than I could control it.

"Me? Well, I have many clients who go here…as you know…and I am invited here often. As for you, this doesn't seem like the type of place a retail salesperson belongs, does it?"

I mentally pleaded with my ego to take his comments in stride.

"Are you a customer of Frankie's?" Jeremy looked toward my date as he asked the question, his narrow, beady eyes honed on Mack, evil rolling off Jeremy.

"He's not—" I said before Mack could interrupt. "He's most certainly not," I double confirmed. I didn't know what Jeremy was trying to insinuate, but I didn't care for it.

"Frances is *with me*. She's my one," Mack said, staring down my ex.

He didn't use the term girlfriend or plus-one or anything trite. I was his *one*…that was what he said. My heart raced in my chest, making me fearful it might explode.

"Take it from me, Frankie is a lot more work than advertised." Jeremy spat out the words.

"I'm sorry, how do you two know one another?" Suddenly the thin brunette spoke, slowly catching on.

"Tell you later, Bridget." Jeremy tried to brush his date off. I recalled him using that trick with me.

"Ex-wife," I told Bridget, looking at her smile fall. She obviously hadn't known Jeremy had been married. I elaborated. "Dated in high school, grew up together, young sweethearts. It didn't work out."

"I quite like the challenge of being with Frances. She's exactly who I need in my life. I'm up to the task," Mack declared. "Now, I'm a member here and I appreciate that you're an invited guest. So please go and have fun, but maintain your distance from us."

"I wanted—" Jeremy started to say.

"We don't care what you want. The man asked you to make yourself scarce." Spencer piped up from the other side of me and made a *go away* sign with his hand.

"Now," Mack emphasized.

I knew my date could be ruthless, but even with his early annoyance at me, I never experienced it happening until this moment. Now, at least I understood how he became so successful. His dominance was palpable.

"Come on, Bridget," was all Jeremy said, wrapping his arm around his date and whisking her away.

As soon as Jeremy was gone, Spencer said, "That guy is an ass. Glad you're not with him, Frances."

He served me a wink, and I felt a connection between us bud. Not a romantic one, something based in admiration and camaraderie—and dealing with Millsy on a regular basis.

"Let's go, Ryan." Spencer tapped his friend on the shoulder. "We can head up to the roof and see what kind of trouble is going on there and let Millsy be with his *one*." Spencer grinned and added, "If you didn't catch on, I like this one," while looking at me.

Ryan nodded and off the pair went. Spencer added a touch of humor to all he said, but he was a good guy, noticing Mack wanted to be with me, and I needed a beat.

With his hand swiping my hair behind my ear, Mack said, "Do you know how beautiful you look tonight? My beautiful Frances, who kickboxed her way into my life."

"Did you mean that? I'm your one?" I couldn't help myself—I needed to ask like I required air to breathe.

He led me to a corner near the window, Mariah Carey now singing "O Holy Night" in the background. "Don't you know that? You're mine,

Frances. In every way. Not one person has been able to make me fall, but you did." His lips brushed my cheek.

"Are you sure it's not Milly and Jimmy rubbing off on us? Some kind of strange sentiment related to them?"

"For sure," he said, firmly. "Their story is sweet and incredibly sad, but not one bit like ours…which is *stalkery*, then happy, and finally very sexy."

He whispered the last part for only me, although no one was paying attention to us other than Bridget on the other side of the room.

"It's all you, Frances. The tiniest woman I know has accomplished the biggest task—captured me. Now, before I take you against this wall for the whole club to witness, can we leave?"

"We didn't eat," I fake-protested.

"We'll send out for something at my place."

"Deli? And then the ice cream?"

"Deli. I know how much you love a turkey, Frances. We'll get whatever you want," he quickly agreed.

Taking my hand, we started to leave. I could feel Jeremy's eyes on my back and sensed him plotting in his mind. On our way to the first floor, I wondered how he would attack Mack because I knew that was coming. It wouldn't matter, because Mack was formidable in a way I was just beginning to understand.

Except as we exited, we had bigger problems.

"How could you?" a woman I knew to be Susie asked Mack, getting up in his personal space. Draped in a full-length mink coat, her cheeks rosy from the wind, she stared at him.

"Hello, Susie," Mack said, pulling out his phone. "Can you text Alex and tell him we're ready?" he asked me while handing over the phone, without looking my way as he put his hand on Susie's elbow, guiding her away from the doorway. It was one of those alpha moments only Mack seemed able to pull off.

"How could you? Go with her? Do this to us?" Susie spoke in a high-pitched tone through gritted teeth. I wasn't even sure how she was accomplishing it.

"What are you going on about?" Mack spat out through clenched teeth. I'd never seen him so venomous.

I listened intently, wanting to know what Mack's aunt was accusing him of… And what did I have to do with any of this?

"Her! Tom recently saw the two of you out to dinner. And being the good guy he is, he asked around who you were canoodling with. And come to find out you're dating this woman—a Burns. His relative… His!" She practically shouted the last part.

My fingers fidgeted and my eyes watched the road for Alex as the fight began to escalate between these two.

"Hey, don't you dare refer to Frances as *this woman*. Show some goddamn respect."

"Why didn't you tell me you knew the granddaughter of the man who made sure I didn't get what I was due? Why? Don't tell me you didn't know when you showed up at my place demanding answers."

What? Alex pulled up, but this was something I didn't know—Susie knew who I was? *And Mack spoke to Susie about my Paps? What did he have to do with what Susie was due?*

"Because I knew you would take issue, that's why. Jimmy Burns wasn't the reason you lost money, Susie. It was all you. You meddled where you weren't supposed to."

"This woman, and I will call her that, is after the same thing her grandfather took from me. She probably heard stories all her life about Milly's rich family. And here she is, befriending you."

Mack's features were tense. I had to still every bone in my body to keep from going to comfort him. He'd kept secrets from me, and now his aunt was badmouthing my grandfather and me on the street. All the embers of our happily-ever-after in my body were snuffed out.

"Susie, shut it. You and I are done here. I'm in love with Frances, and she's not after a damn thing but my heart."

A small flame started to burn, but there wasn't enough kindling for it to grow bright. Once again, I'd fooled myself into thinking something was pure. I thought Mack and I were honest with one another.

"Alex, help Frances into the car," Mack hollered and started to walk toward the passenger seat. Not the back where Alex was opening the door for me.

A chill ran through me, and I welcomed the warmth of the car, despite not understanding why Mack was sitting separate from me.

I sat in the back, hands in my lap, tears trying to burst through the dam I'd mentally put up.

"Take me home," I whispered from the back and Alex nodded.

"Look," Mack turned and spoke, "I have to sit here. I'm too damn mad." He slammed his hand into the dashboard.

Alex didn't even flinch; I assumed he must be used to Mack's outbursts.

Swiveling again, Mack let out a long exhale. "Susie is a bitch. I lied about her knowing. *I* didn't know, but she knew about your grandpa and I uncovered it. I should have told you, but I know how you are on a fact-finding mission and I didn't want her near you."

I felt myself blinking. I guessed we were going to have this discussion with Alex as a witness to the destruction of my heart. "I don't even know her or how she knows me."

"She knew about the first letter in the armoire. She went to see your Paps when I was just a little kid. Like an idiot, she thought she'd win brownie points with Milly. Except it backfired, and Jimmy turned down any efforts to see my grandmother. Not only that, but he also called Milly, and she in turn took away most of what was being left to Susie. Milly arranged for a lump sum and that's it. I knew if I mentioned our involvement, it would only further Susie's hatred toward me, you, your dead grandfather..."

"I thought we were sharing all of our lives with one another. I don't know why. It was silly, but I don't want to hear any more. I never went into this looking for your money…"

"I know," he said. "Will you come back to my place?" He asked softly, looking at me in desperation. His voice cracked and I had a small glimpse at his vulnerability.

I shook my head, and he turned back toward the windshield.

It wasn't until we stopped in front of my building that Mack got out and referenced the last part of his conversation with Susie. Outside, with snow starting to fall around us, he spoke again. "I love you, Frances. I meant it when I said it. I've now hurt you and that's exactly what I was wanting to avoid."

"Good night, Mack."

I couldn't do another heartbreak. I wasn't made for this… I was built for love or nothing at all. I couldn't take heartache.

He stole my hand and pulled me in for a kiss. I turned my head and he placed his lips on my cold cheek.

"I love you," he whispered again.

"Merry…never mind. Happy New Year," was the last thing I said before running inside my building, thinking it would be another Christmas—another year, a lifetime—alone for me.

CHAPTER
Twenty-Four

FRANKIE

He'd called my cell an hour earlier and asked me to come. And like a desperate woman, I ran right out of my apartment. He'd hurt me, yet it felt as if my next breath depended on seeing Mack. I'd been moping, crying, and using eye concealer for the last week.

Faster than I cared to admit, I'd hopped in the elevator and out the door as fresh snow started to flutter in the sky, and jumped into a taxi. It wasn't until we were a few blocks away that I realized I was still wearing ratty gray sweatpants, a purple glitter sweater, and sparkly kitten heels.

It was the festive look I was wearing to dance all the way into next year—on my lonesome. To say I was feeling blue was an understatement.

Of course Mack was waiting for me as I exited the elevator. Standing in the hallway, barefoot and impatient as usual, spiking my heartbeat and warming my cold feet despite his domineering attitude.

"I have to show you something," was all he said as I took two steps toward him, a small smile lifting the corners of his mouth, his gaze taking in my look.

"It's New Year's Eve. You know that, right? Maybe I was going to a party," I snipped, but it was only for effect. My feet took me as far as the threshold and planted themselves firmly in his foyer as I waited for an answer.

He nodded. "I'm glad you weren't."

I raised an eyebrow. "Maybe I was…"

"Of course I know it's New Year's Eve." He ignored my taunt. "Your glitter is cute, but I know you better than that. Those pants clued me in… Maybe you were getting ready to head out?"

This go-round, I opted for a glare. "No, I wasn't going anywhere. A girl can wear whatever she wants to ring in the new year, by herself."

Noting that Mack was speechless, I took in the corner view. Our tree, the one we picked together, was still standing tall in front of the window, its white and pink lights twinkling.

I had no idea what this was about or why he'd summoned me to his place…or why the heck I listened and showed up right away.

"I thought maybe you'd be at a party or in the Hamptons." The accusation rolled off my tongue; it couldn't be helped. Of course I'd been sitting at home, working up a sweat, waiting to open a pint of peppermint bark ice cream. I'd fully restocked on the twenty-sixth, buying every container I could fit in my freezer.

He shook his head.

"You called me over here and then you are mute? What is going on?"

I took in his black joggers, ivory thermal Henley, and bare feet. He looked sexy and scrumptious.

Yet I was utterly confused as Mack took my hand without any more words and walked me toward his bedroom. "Auld Lang Syne" played softly from the speaker in the living area.

We traversed the hallway and a shiver ran down my spine. I hadn't been back since Christmas Eve before the fight that ensued with Susie. I wasn't sure how I'd feel in the actual space, but I couldn't stop my feet from moving.

Continuing in silence, Mack turned the lights on dim and led me to the bed, helping me to sit on the edge.

I was still clueless as to why Mack asked me over, but I didn't think it was for a booty call. As two grown-ass adults, our bedroom experience was hot and fueled by feelings and passion, not for scratching an itch.

"Frances Lily Burns." He said my full name, each syllable full of gravel and emotion. "Thank you for giving me a chance. For coming over when I asked. I knew it was a risk you wouldn't come."

I opened my mouth to ask a question and his finger came to my lips, motioning to stay quiet.

"Shh," he said. "I want you to hear me when I tell you I love you. *I love you, Frances*, and I didn't want to start the next year without you with me. Or any year moving forward. Ever. I wanted to say it here in a quiet place, my focus wholly on you, where there is no doubt to how I feel."

My palms felt clammy entangled with his and he squeezed my hands, making us one.

"For the record, I didn't want to love you. Or anyone, for that matter. And I tried my hardest not to fall for you, but it happened. Actually, I'm pretty sure I dove right off the cliff the very moment you stalked me at the mall, all vim and vigor. You could have brought me to my knees without any kickboxing. You, blond and bold, all of five foot two, bargaining for what you wanted. A hard bargain, I'll say. You could give me a run for my money in the boardroom. And that's one of the many reasons I love you. Your determination, dedication, boundless love, and huge heart."

I took one of my hands out of his and ran my fingers through his thick hair, noting the smallest amount of gray along his temple. "You did say I was dogged."

"That too," he said softly. "I love all of it." He traced my mouth with his thumb. "I love this mouth, even when you're kicking my ass with your wit and snark. I want to kiss that mouth forever, Frances. As you know, that isn't a word I ever used. *Forever* was not for me. But there is no temporary when it comes to you. Not one night or month or even a few years. A lifetime wouldn't be enough time with you."

"Mackenzie." I whispered his full name, the one reserved for the only other woman he'd ever loved—Milly.

"I want you and only you, Frances Lily. Making you happy is my newest mission. Our grandparents died without being their happiest, and I don't want that for you—"

"Or you," I interrupted.

"Us," he responded. He ran his nose along mine. "I'm sorry we fought. I'm ashamed of my family—again. Susie had no right to accuse you of those things, and I know they're not true. She wanted me to get involved with Tom's business contact, and I don't do her bidding. But it doesn't matter who she wants me to be with because I choose you, and her opinion of anyone is inconsequential to me. That being said, she knows if she ever mutters a nasty syllable about you again, I will ruin her." He leaned in and gave me a soft kiss. "Will you have me, Frances? Forever?"

It was just like Mack to lay down a gauntlet like that with Susie and move on with more important business…although I had no idea what he was saying. Was he proposing?

"I need to know you want me as much as I want you. To love and care for, to laugh and cry, to have fun and fight."

I found the words to say, "I don't know what you're asking."

"I'm asking if you'll have me. I want to know if you'll forgive me for my family's mistakes and transgressions. I need to know if you'll allow me to make you happy the best I can. Formal proposal to come later…" He smiled on the last part, his eyes crinkling.

"I never intended to fall for you…or have you fall for me…or take your money," I started.

"Shhh." He repeated his earlier sentiment. "I know. I knew before you ran out of here. And after, but I had to do what my grandmother couldn't do—make it known who I love and choose. You are first in my life, and everyone needed to know that."

"I love you, Mackenzie, and I want to make you happier than you've ever been."

"You already do. Only you, that's all I need."

I ran my hand on his cheek and stared into his gaze.

He tilted closer and ghosted his palm over my stomach. "Well, that's not true. I want to have a baby with you, Frances. I want that with you. If we can."

"Maybe I can't." It was a whisper. I remembered our conversation a month ago when he'd asked if I felt I was missing out on not being a mom.

"We can try. I will be by your side the whole time." He spoke softly. "Nothing you can do will disappoint me. I only want you to have everything in this world."

He was on a jag, a solo mission to appease me and give hope. I already knew him well enough not to try and derail him. I wasn't sure if I could have babies. The doctors hadn't ruled it out, but my late miscarriage had scared me into thinking so. But there was no explaining that to this pigheaded man.

"I'll think about it," was all I said, not admitting that having a baby and failing at that exact pursuit dominated my thoughts ninety percent of the time. I could have included other ideas, like adoption, but it wasn't the time. I knew Mack meant for us to create a life…

"That's enough for me," he whispered.

His mouth was on me before I could say anything more. He slid me up the bed and onto the pillows, kissing me with a fervor we hadn't experienced thus far.

Nuzzling my neck, he brought his palm up my sweater, smoothing along my now warm skin. "I'm digging the look, but can we lose the sweats?"

For a flash, I thought about how quickly I'd forgiven Mack, but I didn't rush over there to fight. I wanted Mackenzie Miller now and always, so I simply said, "Yes."

He yanked my pants down with a whoosh, revealing the fact that I'd also run out of the house without panties.

"Happy New Year to me," was his response.

He slithered down the bed, his tongue immediately finding my heat. He continued to whip me into a frenzy, pausing right before I toppled over well into the next year. In fact, I didn't think he actually slid into me until two or three in the morning—because I graciously returned the oral favor, following in his deliciously teasing efforts.

The next morning, we woke in a tangle of sheets, my glitter sweater strewn about the bed, and Mack asking, "Can you put the heels on? Just the heels?"

This was going to be a fun year, or decade…

MACK

Spencer stood under the canopy of birch branches covered in lace and bright roses and lilies, waiting to marry Frances and me. We took our time as we walked down the aisle together, Frances's arm woven through mine, our heat radiating into one another.

It was a mutual decision to traverse the sandy path like this, both of us realizing we thought the entire "giving someone away" custom was a bit archaic and not necessary, considering our ages. Not to mention Frances didn't want her father intimately involved with the occasion and my dad was gone. A small stroke of luck had Frances's parents on a trip to California during our wedding—it might or might not have been on purpose. As for my mom, we had recently heard she was suffering, and we—Frances, really—decided to help her find a nursing home to live in…and pay for…but that wasn't a story for this day.

This was a monumental day neither Frances nor I thought would ever happen. And here we were.

"We are promising ourselves to each other," was what Frances said when I made sure she didn't want anyone to give her away.

I didn't think I'd ever heard something so pure and honest. "We are making the most special promise," I'd confirmed and meant it.

"But we need a huppah," she'd said, leaving off the *ch* sound. "A huppah canopy is Jewish tradition" she explained.

"Chuppah," I'd corrected, making a clearing sound in my throat as I said the *ch*.

"That's what I said," Frances had countered.

I'd let it go.

"My Paps would have done any custom for his Rosie, and I want to incorporate some traditions from your faith." Her smile had beamed while saying it.

"There's my hopeful little Smurfette," I'd replied, tracing her mouth. She'd punched my arm, and I'd shut up.

Now, we were actually in the moment, and I hoped it was everything Frances imagined.

In the weeks leading up to this, we'd had several conversations on who would marry us and decided against a religious leader. Spencer offered and we said yes. Why not? Not to mention Frances had become a huge fan of my friend and was secretly hoping he asked his supermodel to marry him soon.

Now, we stood looking at one another under the brightly decorated chuppah, the ocean lapping in the background, the heat of the day lingering, holding hands. Ashley stood to the right, holding the bouquet for Frances, while Rachel prepared to introduce us at the reception. I'd finally met Ashley a few months back. And Rachel, being the best friend Frances could ever have, suggested Ashley be the maid of honor. As for me, I didn't need anyone to hold me up; I was a man on the most important assignment of his life.

Frances looked breathtaking in an ivory A-line dress with lace overlay, tiny pink roses interspersed in the pattern. Milly's Chanel bag—the one that brought us together—was on her wrist as her something old. The black was a stark contrast to the gown, but Frances insisted. She also made sure we wrote our own vows, speaking them into existence in front of a very small crowd in the Hamptons, making our love known.

My Dearest Frances,

I think I've been in love with you since the first day you stalked me at the mall. Your green eyes full of life, hope, and promise caught my dulled heart.

For sure, I've been afraid of your kickboxing skills since day one, and have been outsmarted by your tenacious wit every minute since the mall.

I never saw myself in love, but our grandparents loved one another in a way most people can't explain. We unearthed it, and you made it easy to care for you like they felt for one another.

Your smile consumes me and being by your side calms me, comforts me, and shows me a way of being I never knew existed. Being there for you is my most important job.

I promise to love you no matter what and hope you will spend the rest of your life eating fried chicken and mishy-mashy soup and peppermint bark ice cream with me.

"Hopefully not together," she whispered to me. "That's some kind of combination."

"Like us, a weird combo, but perfect," I said quietly, only for Frances. Using my thumb, I swiped a tear from her eye, taking in the grin on her face. "Are you happy, my feisty love?" I spoke softly again, and she nodded.

Mackenzie,

We were not meant to happen. You were supposed to be my partner in crime for a short mission, and somehow you slid into the permanent position. I didn't even know I was taking applications, and you were an unlikely candidate.

Your grandmother and my grandfather are looking down on us and are beyond pleased we found love with one another. With them watching out for us, we are blessed and cherished.

Of course I promise to love you in sickness and health, to try not to ever punch you, and to care for your heart like it deserves to be.

Being with you gives me a sense of completeness I never expected or experienced, and I hope every day is filled with joy. I know there will be pain and hard times, but with you by my side we can conquer anything. Falling in love was our biggest obstacle, and we did a smashing job of it.

I love you, My Dearest Mackenzie.

Spencer instructed us to exchange rings and then Frances turned toward me and stood on her barefoot tiptoes and kissed me first. No instructions to do so, but my woman couldn't wait to get her lips on me.

The kiss was as electric as the first one we shared in my study. And the second one, and every single one after that.

I doubted it would ever change, just as Corey hooted and hollered from the crowd. I didn't expect his exuberance for us to transform either. Nor Connie's, who was watching on livestream. And especially not Teddy's. He stood tall and proud in the second row, his beautiful wife on his arm, both of them smiling. He leaned over and whispered something in Cassandra's ear. I imagined it was about how he always knew this would be, but I'd never believed him.

I didn't.

Except here I was, with photos of Milly and Jimmy set on a table behind Spencer, staring back at Frances and me. I knew my newfound forever was because of the older couple and for them too. They never had this—two people in love, no holds barred, nothing between them, differing backgrounds and opinions appreciated while a new future was in bloom.

All you had to do was ask Frances about my suggesting she sell women's clothing rather than men's and the fight that ensued. I didn't like sharing her with other men, but that wasn't my choice. Apparently Frances was never quitting her job and it was part of the fabric of our lives.

Although I hoped she might be taking some time off soon…

* * * * * * * * *

FIVE MONTHS LATER

"One more push," the doctor said, and my tiny wife growled.
"I can't…"

"Let's fucking go," I half whisper-shouted. Yes, it was stupid of me to say, and I knew it before Frances gave me a death stare and squeezed my hand hard enough to send shivers through my whole body. I did that a lot, said stupid shit.

"I'm going to punch you."

"You promised not to, in our vows," I reminded her.

"Let's fucking go. *You* push a baby out of your body," she said through gritted teeth and did as the doctor said—pushed.

Frances was not letting up. This was going to be the last push if she had anything to do with it. And I knew my wife. She got what she wanted.

We'd realized we were pregnant about two months before the wedding. Frances had missed a period and without my knowing went to the doctor. Panicked over bad omens and her ex, she kept the results to herself for two weeks until I dragged it out of her, after she was acting strange at kickboxing.

Originally, she'd fallen asleep during her beloved spy show, and that was my first clue. Then she'd requested an egg salad sandwich on sourdough with extra pickles. It was an order I'd never heard her make,

and my second tip-off. Then came the teary-eyed look at kickboxing…
It was the exact opposite of no-holds-barred Frankie.

Of course, she didn't want to say a thing to anyone about the pregnancy, and I agreed. After what happened way back when, she was in charge of how we handled everything.

We hid the pregnancy through our honeymoon in Grand Cayman, and then as long as we could. Without my asking, Frances took the last three months off work.

Of course, Susie gave her a snide comment about it, remarking, "Oh really? Already letting my nephew take care of you…" and I hadn't spoken to her since. Tom called a few times with business ideas, and Corey was instructed to take a message.

At close to forty, Frances felt this was her last chance, and she wanted this baby more than she even let me see. She would do anything to protect the fragile soul inside her—in a way my mother never could.

"I'm so lucky to have you," I said.

With those words, my wife gave one more giant grunt that could have rivaled any bear in nature. James Rose Miller was born at a few minutes after two in the morning. With a ton of blond hair and rosy cheeks like her namesake, my daughter, Jamie, had a set of lungs on her.

About the Author

Rachel Blaufeld writes *Second Chance* at Love Stories.

A recent poll of her readers described her as *insightful, generous, articulate,* and *spunky.* Originally a social worker, Rachel creates broken yet redeeming characters. She's been known to turn up the angst like cranking up the heat in the dead of winter.

As a side note, Blaufeld, also a long-time blogger and an advocate of woman-run anything, is fearless about sharing her opinion. To her, work/life/family balance is an urban legend, but she does her best.

Rachel has also blogged for *The Huffington Post, Modern Mom,* and *USA TODAY,* where she shared conversations at "In Bed with a Romance Author" and reading recommendations at "Happily Ever After."

Rachel lives around the corner from her childhood home in Pennsylvania with her family and two beagles. Her obsessions include running, coffee, basketball, icing-filled doughnuts, antiheroes, and mighty fine epilogues.

www.ingramcontent.com/pod-product-compliance
Lightning Source LLC
Chambersburg PA
CBHW050526260626
47157CB00004B/1490